Swan Song

Takeaways

COLIN THIELE

Swan Song

Lothian
BOOKS

Thomas C. Lothian Pty Ltd
132 Albert Road, South Melbourne, Victoria 3205
www.lothian.com.au

National Library of Australia
Cataloguing-in-publication data:

Thiele, Colin,1920- .
Swan song.

For children ages 8-12.
ISBN 0 7344 0325 9 (pbk).

1. Swans - Juvenile fiction. 2. Wildlife conservation - South Australia -
Coorong National Park - Juvenile fiction. 3. Coorong National Park
(S. Aust.) - Juvenile fiction. I. Title. (Series : Takeaways).

A823.3

Cover and interior illustrations by Robert Ingpen
Cover design by Sandra Nobes
Book design by Paulene Meyer
Printed in Australia by Griffin Press

One

'You won't be going to school this year,' Mitch's mother said. 'You'll be doing your lessons at home.'

The news was so unexpected that Mitch gulped. 'Why?' he asked.

'Because they've cancelled the school bus.'

'Who has?'

'The Government. The other children who used the bus last year have all moved away. You're the only one left. Nobody is going to run a bus all that way just for one person. So you'll work at home.'

'All the year?'

'This year and next year. After that we'll have to send you to high school in the city.'

All kinds of ideas were racing about in Mitch's head. His life had always been so simple and well arranged but now everything had suddenly exploded. He had expected to start the year at school in Room 4 with Old Swamp. That was what everyone called Mr Marshland. Mitch thought it was a good nickname.

A new idea crossed his mind and he smiled slyly. 'I won't have to get up so early any more, will I — if I don't have to catch the bus? I'll be able to sleep in.'

His mother was curt. 'Indeed you won't.'

Mitch was starting to like the idea of staying at home every day. 'I'll be able to do my schoolwork whenever I like. Go fishing if I want. I won't have a teacher watching me all the time.'

His mother fixed him with a stern stare. '*I'll* be watching you all the time. There'll be no fishing until every last bit of your schoolwork is finished for the day. I'll see to that.'

Mitch hung his head. What his mother said was true, all right. She would probably be tougher than any teacher he had ever had. He looked at her questioningly. 'How will I know what I have to do?'

'You'll get everything you need from Distance Education. They'll send you the lessons and mark your work. And every now and then a teacher will come down to see how you're getting on. She'll explain the hard bits and show me how I can help you.'

Mitch began to see that life without school-rooms and classmates was not going to be free and easy after all.

Two

Mitch's full name was Mitchell but nobody ever used it. He was Mitch to everyone — the bus driver, the school secretary, the teachers, even his own family. It was the same with his father whose name was Foster but who was always called Fos. Those who knew his full name — Foster Bird — thought it was incredibly apt because he was a ranger at the Coorong National Park in South

Australia and one of his jobs was to foster the life of the birds and other wildlife there. He was a strong, active man, very firm and thorough, and always neatly dressed in his ranger's uniform. Mitch's mother was Meg, short for Margaret. She was kind but as sharp as a tack. If Mitch tried to argue with her he usually lost the argument.

They lived in a house on the high ground overlooking the long stretch of the Coorong lagoon — a hundred kilometres of it stretching far away to left and right. When they looked out at it from one room or another, the different views framed by the windows were like the loveliest paintings Mitch could ever imagine. And they changed from hour to hour according to the time of the day.

Just below them the ragged shore ran away into the distance. The lagoon, a little more than a kilometre wide just there, stretched straight ahead, and beyond it the jumbled crests of the sandhills rose up on the peninsula that separated the Coorong from the open sea. A wild place it was, with long rollers sweeping in from the far south and thundering onto the beach with a never-ending roar.

Sometimes in the early morning when Mitch stood watching from the window of his room, the water in the Coorong was so calm that it lay before him like a huge mirror. At other times, when the breeze blew like a gentle breath and rucked up tiny wavelets, the mirror turned into ripple glass, brightened by sunlight or dulled by passing clouds. And when fierce winds blasted the peninsula in the distance the sand was whipped from the top of the sandhills until it trailed away in thin streams like golden smoke.

Mitch was happy to look out at the scene forever. Often it was made even more magical by great flocks of waterbirds that lived on the Coorong or came to visit it from distant places. Although he didn't especially think about it, Mitch knew he was lucky to be living in a place like that.

Three

*B*ecause it was still early in January, Mitch didn't have to worry about schoolwork for another two or three weeks and was able to do what he liked best — pottering about on the Coorong. Sometimes he helped his father on patrol but most of the time he was on his own. He was allowed to use one of his father's boats — a little dinghy with an outboard motor. It gave him freedom to putter up and down on the lagoon, sometimes pausing at a good spot to catch fish for a while, sometimes landing to explore the nearby shore, and now and again sailing over to the peninsula and walking across the sand-hills to the ocean beach. There he collected dozens of cockles — big juicy cockles that were perfect for bait and for eating — and put them in a wet sack to keep them fresh on the trip back. It was a long walk, and he was usually tired out at the end of it.

His mother and father had very strict rules for him when he went out on his own like that. 'Take care and always think ahead,' his father said over and over. 'Even though it doesn't look like it, the Coorong can be a dangerous place. A sudden storm can sink your boat in a second. Always put up markers when you go over to the beach. The walk across the sandhills may only be a kilometre or two but you can get lost there all the same. And never go into the sea on your own. Never ever, not even in water up to your knees. There are rips and surges, and huge rollers thundering in without warning. They're so strong that they could sweep an elephant away. You'd just be a bit of flotsam, drowned in a wink. So always watch what you're doing. Careful. Careful. Careful. That's your motto.'

Once, when he did lose his way for a while he was glad that his father had drummed such safety lessons into him because he was able to find the markers he had driven into the sand and follow them back to the dinghy where he had left it moored by the shore.

There were always interesting things to explore on the ocean beach, or unlikely surprises to stumble on — driftwood washed up along the high tide mark, a fisherman's coloured buoy, a sodden wicker basket half buried in the sand, pieces of rope, a craypot, beautiful shells, and even an oar that must have been washed overboard from a trawler in a storm.

There were also interesting things to discover in the sandhills — blackened stones from the ancient campfires of the Aboriginal people, and masses of shells from their seafood heaped up over thousands of years in piles called middens; dead birds that had been wounded far away during the duck shooting season and had struggled on until they had fallen and died among the sandhills; and poisonous snakes that had to be avoided slowly and carefully.

Sometimes rubbish from campers lay scattered about — empty stubbies, bottles and flagons, cardboard cartons, coloured wrappers, maggoty bits of meat or fish, chicken bones, plastic bags, cans and tins, and even thongs and bits of clothing that the campers had overlooked, probably because they'd been too drunk to put them on. When he found disgusting litter like that Mitch put up markers to pinpoint the spot so that he and his father could go back to clean up the mess and search for clues that might lead them to the yahoos who had done it.

Four

$\mathcal{O}$ne day at low tide, when he had just finished collecting a bag of cockles on the beach, Mitch heard the roar of far-off engines. He looked up quickly and was just able to see two dark specks in the distance — dune buggies or four-wheel-drive jalopies with hyped-up motors — hurtling towards him like demented metal hornets.

Mitch grabbed his bag, raced across the beach,

and hid behind a bush at the edge of the sandhills. He was only just in time. The two buggies were travelling so fast that they flashed past him in a couple of seconds and dwindled away in the distance. He had only a fleeting glimpse of the drivers. The one in the lead seemed to be a big man with a beard, his eyes hidden behind dark goggles. He wasn't wearing a helmet of any kind and his long hair streamed back in the wind of his speed. The second driver was hunched low, concentrating madly on the buggy in front, straining to keep up. Mitch saw no more than a red helmet, a blue shirt, and two arms clutching the steering wheel. Within seconds both of the buggies were distant specks again, although the roar of their engines still hung in the air.

Mitch came out of his hiding place onto the beach and stared after them. The tide was out and the strip of smooth sand between the sandhills and the sea was marked with their tyre treads so clearly that the pattern seemed to have been stitched onto it. He could understand why the place was called the Ninety Mile Beach, and why it was so popular with petrol heads. No race track could have been more inviting.

He had just decided to head for home when he caught the sound of their engines again. They had turned round and were on their way back. He didn't want to be seen, and he certainly didn't want to be run down by a couple of hoons, so he raced back into the sandhills and crouched with his knees bent, peering over a small ridge as the two shapes rocketed towards him again. He hoped that this time he would be able to see them more clearly or perhaps catch a glimpse of their registration numbers — if they had any. But when the buggies were within a hundred metres of him they suddenly swerved to the right in a great blast of sand and disappeared into the sandhills. Their engines howled and they slowed to a crawl as they bucked and rocked up the crests and down the dips until he lost them somewhere deep in the peninsula.

Mitch took his bag of cockles and followed their tracks for a while. It looked as though feral pigs had been rooting about. Deep troughs had been gouged in the sand, and where some of the crests were held together by fragile plants the tyres, straining for traction, had uprooted them and flung them aside.

Mitch eyed the tracks in disgust. He knew what would happen next. When the winter gales howled in from the south they would blow the loose sand forward and start a blow-out. Without the roots of the plants to bind the crests the sand-hills would 'start marching', as his father said, creating a little Sahara and pushing right into the Coorong.

That night at the tea table Mitch described what had happened. His mother shook her head angrily. 'Thoughtless nincompoops. They haven't got a brain between them.'

His father grunted. 'They're so empty-headed that if you shone a torch into their ears their eyes would light up.'

They all laughed at that but it was a sour laugh. 'It's vandalism,' Fos said, 'but it's hard to prevent. We have to catch them red-handed in pro-hibited places to prosecute them. The law isn't really strict enough to protect the environment properly.'

'Those two were going so fast that you'd need a helicopter to catch up with them,' Mitch said. 'Just to find out who they were.'

His father snorted. 'I can guess who they were, just from your description'.

'Who?'

'Mr Hairy Beard would be Hardy Blight. He's massive. Looks like a sumo wrestler. His offsider is Jimmy Small. Small by name and small by brain. They always hang out together. The Big and the Little.'

'Luckily most drivers aren't like that,' Meg said. 'They're sensible and keep to the permitted places.'

'Yes, but you only need one or two hoboes to do the damage.'

Mitch remembered his father's description of the two drivers. If he ever saw Hardy Blight and Jimmy Small again he hoped he would be able to recognise them.

Five

Mitch liked going out with his father, who knew enough about the Coorong to fill a dozen books. A day with him was a sort of lesson — a quiet lesson, so enjoyable that Mitch didn't even realise how much he was learning.

They usually talked about the natural creatures, especially the birds. There were thousands of them, of so many different kinds that Mitch would never have been able to write down the details about even half of them.

One day when they were standing side by side on a sandhill overlooking the Southern Ocean his father pointed to a couple of birds on the beach below. 'Do you recognise those two?'

Mitch peered. 'Hooded plovers.'

'Yes. Birds like that are in danger from buggies when they nest on the beach.'

'And get run over?'

'Yes, especially the fledglings because they hide in patches of weed. Even if they're not hurt they're frightened and disturbed. And the eggs in the nests get crushed.' His father paused. 'But I guess Mr Bonehead Blight wouldn't be too concerned about that.'

'Are there many plovers around here?'

'Not enough, but we're trying to build them up. Human beings are not the only creatures that threaten them. We've baited a lot of foxes and feral cats on the peninsula. That helps too.'

They walked back over the sandhills to their boat moored on the Coorong and sailed slowly up the lagoon for an hour or two. There were waterbirds everywhere — pelicans with big paunches, graceful black swans, cormorants, ducks, sand-pipers, stilts … In certain places where fresh water seeped out of the sandhills near the shore, great flocks had gathered waiting for a drink because the Coorong itself was often saltier than the sea. 'You'd find it hard to sink in some parts of the Coorong,' Mitch's father joked, 'no matter how hard you tried.'

Some distance further on they came to a place where hundreds of wading birds were pottering about in shallow water near the shore.

'Sandpipers,' Mitch said.

His father nodded. 'Some of the best long-distance flyers in the world. They would have come down from the Arctic last October — a little trip of 10,000 kilometres or so across the globe. They'll feed up here until April and then fly back again. And so it goes on, year after year.

Mitch gazed at the birds in wonder. 'It's a bit of a miracle, to fly across the world like that, just to come here every year?'

'It's magic,' his father answered. 'And there are hundreds of miracles like that going on around us every day.'

Six

Mitch's carefree life came to an end on the last day of January. His mother had a phone call to say that a teacher from Distance Education was coming to explain the year's arrangements and go through the details of Mitch's program. Her name was Mrs Mary Penn.

Mitch was uneasy when he saw her car pull up in the yard on the following morning. He had been

trying to guess what sort of person she would be —
tall or short, young or old, blonde or dark-haired,
lively or stern. He didn't have to wait long to find
out. She parked the car, took out a box and a big
briefcase from the back of the car, and headed for
the house. Mitch hid behind the curtains at the
front window and peered at her nervously. He was
glad that she didn't look grumpy and fed up, or
come marching forward like a military officer.

Mitch's mother met her at the door and called
him over to be introduced. Mrs Penn shook his
hand firmly and beamed at him. 'Mitchell,' she said.
'I've been wanting to meet you.'

He was surprised at the sound of his full
name. It was the first time he had heard it in years.
Mrs Penn kept smiling at him. She gave the impression that this moment was one of the highlights
of her life.

'We must get to know each other,' she said,
'because we're going to be working together for the
rest of the year.' She eyed him kindly. 'I'm sure we're
both going to enjoy it.'

Mitch began to fear that she was too much of
a talker, one of those people who go on and on,

suffocating their listeners with words. He'd had a teacher like that once before. But he soon realised that it was just her way of breaking the ice. After he and his mother had been sitting down with her at the table for an hour he began to like her. She was fun, full of jokes and little stories, but clear and firm when she needed to be.

Bit by bit she went through everything Mitch had to do: his regular daily program, essays, projects and assignments, research work, books for information, resources on the Internet, rules, schedules, and the deadlines by which his tasks had to be finished and sent in to her. There was also a hotline by phone, fax or e-mail if he needed something urgently. Mrs Penn paused at last and smiled again. 'And if necessary your mother will be right here to help you.'

The work seemed to be piling up like Mount Everest as more and more books, papers and folios kept coming out of her briefcase. He murmured and nodded when she asked him whether he understood, but in his heart he was sure he wouldn't be able to remember half of it.

Luckily at midday his father came home from

a meeting with some Coorong fishermen and decided to stay for lunch. It was a happy hour, with lots of talk and laughter around the table. Mitch watched Mrs Penn the whole time and decided that she was rather like his mother — about the same age and shape, with the same sort of hair, the same looks and the same nature. The two of them were getting on so well that Mitch was delighted she had been chosen to be his teacher for the year.

Later in the afternoon when she packed up and prepared to leave she turned to Mitch again and shook his hand. 'Goodbye, Mitchell, and good luck. Don't hesitate to call me if you need help with anything at all. I'll always be in touch, and I'll come down to visit you again later in the year.' She paused. 'So now it's up to you. Your program begins on Monday.' She smiled broadly.' But you can start earlier if you like.'

Mitch's mother looked at him steadily 'He will. He'll start tomorrow morning. At eight o'clock sharp.'

Seven

$\mathcal{B}$efore long Mitch began to like working on his own. He found that he could finish most of his assignments ahead of time, and he did more than he needed to if he really enjoyed the topic. Mrs Penn was impressed and sent back encouraging messages.

Mitch was also lucky that his mother and father were always handy. His mother loved reading and she helped him all the time with subjects like English and History. He was amazed at the things she knew about books, writers and historical events. His father liked mathematics, science and technology. He used his computer constantly to record and analyse details about the Coorong environment. He could explain at a glance how to solve the maths problems on Mitch's work sheets, and if Mitch asked for help with science questions he could usually answer them out of his head.

Early in the term Mitch was asked to do a research project on a topic of his own choice. He chose wetlands and waterbirds, and he found it so interesting that he prepared a big folder about it, including the proper scientific names for the birds and adding lots of detail about their food, nests, eggs, habits and the threats to their environment by human beings.

He persuaded his father to take him out in the Government patrol boat to photograph as many of the Coorong waterbirds as they could. In the end he had a beautiful collection of pictures — birds in flight, birds wading, birds swimming, birds standing on the shore, birds singly or in flocks. Mrs

Penn was so impressed when he sent his folder to her that she wrote a special letter. 'This is one of the best projects I have ever seen,' she said. 'It is so good that it ought to be preserved. Please keep it in a safe place.' Mitch was prouder than a peacock.

He had so much help from Mrs Penn and from his mother and father that his schoolwork was easier than he had expected. He usually finished the day's program early in the afternoon and had time to go fishing if he wanted to, or mend a broken rod, or mess about with his camera. And now and then he could still go over to the ocean beach or explore the sandhills on the peninsula.

One day Mrs Penn wrote 'You are one of the luckiest persons alive to be living where you are. I'd love to live in a place like that.'

Mitch agreed.

Eight

The Coorong was never quite the same from season to season or from year to year. It changed from winter to summer, and sometimes it changed because something unusual happened. If the River Murray came down in flood the huge barrages at the river mouth had to be opened and torrents of fresh water thundered out into the nearby reaches. If there was a very high tide that surged in from the sea, or very strong winds blowing onshore, the water in the Coorong was likely to rise. And in the heat of summer much of the far end of the south lagoon evaporated, leaving oozy mudflats and rotting plants that sent out an awful stench.

After Mitch had been working on his own for a while, and everything in the Bird household was running smoothly, one of these changes began to happen. The water in the Coorong began to rise — not much, but enough to make a difference. In a roundabout way it changed Mitch's life forever.

His father tested the water in different places and kept an eye on things in the National Park and the sanctuary. 'I think I'd better take a look at Pelican Island,' he said one morning, 'just to see what's going on down there.'

Mitch's eyes brightened. 'Can I come too?'

His father hesitated. 'Better check with your mother first. Have you finished your schoolwork?'

'Sure. Anyway it's Saturday, so there isn't any.'

Mitch knew that if it had been a weekday his mother would never have agreed, but she was usually more lenient at the weekend.

'OK, you can go,' she said, 'but not before you've cleaned your room. It's disgusting. Makes me sick to look at it.'

'No worries.' Mitch worked so fast, making his bed, tidying his desk and putting away his clothes, that he reckoned he should have used a stopwatch to record the time in the Guinness Book of Records. 'Right, let's go,' he called.

They loaded the dinghy and the outboard onto the boat trailer and hitched it behind the Land Cruiser because it was more sensible to drive down the highway and launch the boat at a convenient spot rather than sail laboriously all the way down the Coorong. A cluster of half a dozen tiny islands near Pelican Island were special nesting places for the birds, especially pelicans. All the islands and the water for about a hundred metres around them were prohibited places. Only rangers and people with permits were allowed to go there.

Mitch and his father launched the boat and set off. They kept at a distance for a while to avoid frightening the birds with the engine's racket, but then they cut the motor and used the oars. Even before they beached the dinghy and stepped ashore on Pelican Island they guessed that something was wrong.

'Things don't look good,' Mr Bird said. 'Something has happened.'

Mitch was uneasy. 'What?'

'The place is almost deserted.'

'Why?'

'I don't know.'

They started to walk forward. There were nests everywhere but hardly any adult pelicans.

'Abandoned,' Mitch's father said. 'Almost all of them.'

Mitch was shocked. In nest after nest he could see tiny dead pelicans, or eggs left cold and lifeless.

'The grown-ups have really gone?' he asked in disbelief.

'Yes.'

'But why?'

'Who knows. A virus or disease, saltier water, less food, predators.'

'And they left the babies to die?'

'Evidently'.

Mitch couldn't believe it. 'That's awful.'

'Nature is like that, Mitch. It has happened before. Years ago more than a thousand young pelicans were left to die because of rising water.'

'That's horrible.'

His father sighed. 'That's life.' He hesitated. 'Or death.'

'You'd think the parents would have done something to save them.'

'What could they do? They couldn't very well take them in their beaks and carry them away, like a cat with kittens.'

'They could have tried.'

'They'll come back and nest again. Luckily this sort of thing doesn't happen very often.'

They walked on slowly, looking this way and that. A few metres further on they found a nest that still had some life in it — two tiny pelicans huddled together and looking up soundlessly with their beaks open.

Mr Bird stopped short. 'Incredible. They've just been abandoned by the look of it.'

Mitch knelt down beside the nest and cupped the tiny bodies in his hand.

He looked up. 'What are we going to do

with them, Dad? We can't just leave them here to die.'

His father eyed him sadly. 'They'll probably die anyway, no matter what we do. They need food and warmth straight away.'

'But we have to do something to save them.'

'What can we do?'

'We could take them home. I could look after them until they're big enough to live on their own.'

'And feed them all the time? Do you know how much pelicans eat each day?'

'I'll catch fish for them. I caught a lot of mullet yesterday. They're still in the fridge. I'll cut them up into little pieces and feed the babies bit by bit.'

His father shook his head. 'They won't survive, Mitch. You'd have one chance in a million of saving them.'

'But I could try. That would be better than just walking away and leaving them here to starve.'

'I know it's sad, but ...'

'Please, Dad.'

His father gave in at last. 'Well, all right, but don't be too disappointed when they die.'

Mitch was ecstatic. 'Thanks, Dad. I'll save them, you'll see.'

He took off his pullover and wrapped the two tiny bodies snugly in the folds. Then he urged his father to set off for home as fast as he could.

Nine

The task of saving the two pelicans started as soon as they arrived back at the house. At first Mitch's mother was unhappy about it, but when she saw them lying there helplessly she pitied them so much that she agreed to help. They found a box and turned it into a warm nest with bits of woollen cloth, and Mitch took a fish from the fridge and started to cut it up.

'Those pieces are too big,' his mother said. 'Each piece has to be smaller than your little finger nail.'

It was a critical moment. Mitch knew that if the pelicans were already too weak to eat they would be dead before morning. They could barely raise their heads. Most of the time they lay silently, too feeble to move. He took a tiny fragment of fish, lifted the head of the first pelican, and coaxed it with the morsel. It didn't respond. He tried again and again but failed every time.

His mother stood watching sadly. After a while she shook her head. 'It's no use, Mitch. I'm afraid you've lost them.'

'No,' Mitch answered stubbornly. 'We can't just let them die. We have to keep trying.'

'Then try feeding the other one. Perhaps he's a bit stronger.'

Mitch took the second pelican and helped it to sit up. It opened its bill feebly, waiting to be fed. Mitch's heart skipped. He took the morsel of fish and popped it in. It was swallowed in a wink. 'Look,' he cried. 'Look, look. He's eating.' He offered the open beak another bit, and then another and another. They all disappeared quickly.

Mitch glanced up at his mother. 'He's hungry all right.'

'Starving.'

'I hope I've got enough fish.'

'Don't give him too much or you'll kill him with kindness. He has to build up his strength slowly.'

'OK.' He put down the bowl he was holding even though the little beak was still clamouring for more.

'Try the other one again,' his mother suggested.

They both watched anxiously as he tried coaxing it again and again but it seemed too weak to respond.

'It's sad,' Mrs Bird said at last. 'I think he's given up. He's smaller than his brother.'

'I have to keep trying.'

'You can't go on for ever.'

'I'll keep going for a while anyway.'

He was about to give up and walk away when the little pelican moved its head briefly and opened its beak. Mitch was so surprised that for a moment he fumbled the bit of fish he was holding and almost missed his chance. He managed to pop it in at the last instant and watched breathlessly. After a moment's pause it was gone and then, miraculously, the beak opened again, wanting more.

Mitch was in such a hurry to seize the chance that he upended the bowl and spilled bits of fish all over the place. Luckily it didn't affect the pelican. It swallowed the second bit, and the third, eating more and more eagerly. Mitch's hopes rose. Now there was at least some chance that he might be able to save both of them.

All through the afternoon and evening he kept going back to give them a few more tidbits until his mother grew impatient and sent him off to bed. But he was up again before daybreak, hurrying over to the box to see if they were still alive. He held his breath as he peered inside. They were huddled together in a corner but they both stirred and raised their heads as he watched. 'They're alive,' he yelled. 'Both of them are alive.'

His mother came over and smiled. 'Good.'

'I'm amazed,' his father said. 'I didn't think they'd last the night.'

'I'll save them now.'

'Don't be too sure, there's still a long way to go.'

'They'll be OK. I'll feed them all the time. I'll catch lots of fish, enough to last for a whole week.'

His mother eyed him severely. 'Don't think you're going fishing every day. Your job is to do schoolwork, not breed pelicans.'

'Ah heck, Mum,' Mitch answered. 'One of Dad's jobs is to save all the wildlife. I'm just helping him.'

His mother rolled her eyes and went into the kitchen.

Ten

A week went by before Mitch was really confident the pelicans were going to live. They were bigger and stronger now, and they ate greedily whenever he came to feed them. His father, who had been sceptical all along, was not only surprised but unhappy.

'They're going to be an albatross around your neck for the rest of your life', he warned.

Mitch knew what his father meant but he pretended to misunderstand.

'They're pelicans, not albatrosses.'

'Don't be dense. They'll be a burden. They'll depend on you for ever.'

'It's my job to feed them.'

'You're overfeeding them.'

'They were starving. I have to build them up while the fish are plentiful.'

His father eyed the bigger pelican. 'I don't know about the fish,' he joked, 'but that fellow is certainly plenty full.'

Meg hooted with laughter. 'Now we know what to call him.'

Mitch laughed too. 'Plenty Full?'

'Yes. It suits him, don't you think? He's growing a paunch already.

Mitch pointed. 'And what about the little one?'

'He's not plenty full, that's for sure,' his father answered. 'More like plenty empty.'

'Plenty Empty?' Mitch repeated, rolling about with laughter. 'That's cool, Dad.'

The names stuck. From that moment the two pelicans were called Plenty Full and Plenty Empty.

Eleven

The arrival of Plenty Full and Plenty Empty was not the only event to shake the Bird household. Before long Mitch caused another upheaval.

He was sailing up the Coorong looking for a good fishing spot. He needed to build up a big supply so that the pelicans would have enough to eat when he was busy or when the weather was bad. He sailed closer to the shore than usual, cruising slowly with the outboard throttled back. There was shallow water ahead with reeds that were likely to snag his line.

He was about to veer out into clearer water when he caught sight of a heap of stems and grasses arranged in a rough circle about a metre wide. It was clear that something had built it there, anchored in a weedy patch. Mitch guessed at once what it was — a swan's nest like dozens of others he had seen on his outings with his father. He cut the engine and edged closer with the oars to get a better view, unsure whether it was still being used.

He was surprised by what he found — a single greenish-white egg lying on swansdown in the middle of the nest. Normally he would have expected to see four or five eggs in a cluster, or a group of tiny, newly-hatched cygnets huddled together. He wondered where the parents had gone. Normally they wouldn't leave the nest for long. They were far more likely to stay and defend it fiercely, hissing and rushing forward to drive away intruders.

Something must have upset them or driven

them away, leaving just one egg. Perhaps it was a fox or some other predator because the nest was only a few metres from the shore. There was no other reason Mitch could think of, unless they had died of disease. Plenty of food was growing in the water nearby — the kind of grass everyone called widgeon grass, although its real name was ruppia. It grew a kind of tuber down in the mud which the swans liked to eat. Mitch had often seen them up-end themselves and reach down with their long necks to probe about for the tubers or leafy bits of the grass.

He pushed on until he was close enough to reach out and touch the egg. It was cool to the touch — not cold enough to stop it from hatching, but certainly not as warm as it should be. Clearly it had been abandoned.

Mitch sat gazing at the egg. He was in a quandary. Should he save it by taking it home, or just leave it where it was? It was a crime to interfere with wildlife in the Coorong but what if a little cygnet was about to hatch? It would be horribly cruel to go away and leave it to die.

He sat hesitating, wondering what to do. It was a hard decision but in the end he made up his mind. He picked up the egg, wrapped it in a piece of cloth, and set off for home.

Twelve

When his father discovered what Mitch had done he was furious. 'You haven't got the brains of a bread-crumb,' he stormed. 'First it was pelicans, now it's swans. Surely you know by now that you shouldn't interfere with wildlife. You should not interfere. Not ever.'

Mitch was red faced and close to tears. 'Yes, but ...'

His father cut him off. 'Don't "yes but" me. It was an idiotic thing to do. There are big fines for that sort of stupidity.'

Mitch hurried to have his say before his father thundered at him again. 'I thought the baby in the egg would die, that's all.'

'You don't think ahead, Mitch. How many times have I told you that? Even if you hatch the egg and save the swan, what are you going to do with it? You'll be shackled with it for the rest of your life. You've already got two pelicans to feed for ever. And you could be fined thousands of dollars if someone reported it.'

'I'm sorry, Dad,' Mitch stammered. I just wanted to …'

'And what kind of patsy would I look? Can you imagine the headlines? WILDLIFE CRIME: RANGER'S SON FINED. That would be great, wouldn't it?'

Mitch suddenly saw why his father was so upset. It was not just that he was concerned about the swan, although that was true enough. It was the possible damage to his good name, and to his position as a ranger.

'You can guess the story someone like Hardy Blight would make of it,' he added. 'He'd broadcast it all over the place. I warned him about his dune buggy the other day so he'd love to hit back at me.'

'I'm sorry, Dad,' Mitch repeated weakly. 'I didn't think it would …'

'No, you didn't think.'

A tear welled in the corner of Mitch's eye and trickled down beside his nose. There was nothing more he could say. He just had to stand silently and bear his father's outburst until it dwindled into a rumble and finally ended. Mitch's mother stood listening. She felt some of Mitch's pain with him. Although she knew well enough that what he had done was foolish and wrong, she thought there was no point in going on and on about it.

She turned to her husband. 'Now that the egg is here it would be just as wrong to throw it away and smash it. Mitch might as well try to hatch it and see what happens.'

Fos made a rumbling sound at the back if his throat. 'Well, if you must.' He turned on Mitch. 'But never do anything like that again. Not ever.' And he walked out of the room.

Mitch felt like hugging his mother. He was sure she was the kindest and most sensible person in the world. He wiped his eyes and went to get the egg. 'How am I going to hatch it?' he asked. 'I hadn't thought of that.'

She wagged her finger at him. 'Try not to say "I hadn't thought" or "I didn't think".' It sounded stern but she said it with half a smile. 'To incubate the egg you'll have to keep it warm at a nice even temperature.'

'How can I do that?'

She smiled again. 'Let's both think.'

In the end she came up with a shrewd suggestion. In the shed they found an old table lamp that was used in the days before electricity. It had a heavy base that was really a brass tank for kerosene, a wick that could be moved up and down, and a glass chimney to protect the flame. When the lamp was alight, the air above the chimney was always nice and warm.

They built a wire stand that surrounded the lamp, and fixed a small metal platform on top of it, ten or twelve centimetres above the chimney. Finally they made a nest of woollen cloth on the platform and snuggled the egg into it.

'Eureka,' Mitch's mother said. 'The new Mitchell Bird incubator. State of the art. Brilliant.'

For the first time that day Mitch laughed. He loved his mother even more.

'From now on you'll have to watch it carefully,' she said. 'Keep up the supply of kerosene and check the wick. If the flame is too low the egg will get cold, but if it's too high you'll cook it.'

'I'll be really really, careful,' Mitch answered. 'I'll watch it all the time.'

'No you won't. You'll do your schoolwork *all the time*. You'll just check the lamp now and then.'

Although Mitch was grateful for his mother's kindness his heart was still raw from the way his father had shouted at him. It was even harder to bear because his father was normally a fair man, always willing to answer his questions or take him out for lessons in the wildlife sanctuary. It wasn't until later that night that Mitch began to understand his father's outburst. He was doing some homework in his room (they called it homework even though all his schoolwork was homework, no matter whether he did it during the day or night) and his mother and father were talking in the kitchen. Most of the time their voices were just a background murmur that meant nothing to Mitch, until he happened to overhear the name Hardy Blight. He sat up and listened closely.

'The maddening thing about it,' his father was saying, 'is that it's impossible to charge them unless you've got evidence. The law wants witnesses, witnesses, witnesses. If someone drives through the place like an army tank, scours out tracks in all directions, leaves litter lying everywhere until the place looks like the local garbage dump, the police can't arrest anyone unless we can prove who did it.'

After that outburst Mitch heard his mother's gentle voice. 'Are you sure it was Hardy Blight?'

'Yes. Absolutely.'

'But the police haven't charged him?'

'No, there's no proof.'

'And you can't get it?'

'Not unless we can find witnesses who actually saw him doing it.'

His father snorted. 'But at least he knows that we're watching him. I met him at the roadhouse today and asked him whether he had seen the damage in some of the best places in the Park. New tracks. Bushes uprooted. Litter. And do you know what he said?'

'What?'

Mitch heard his father growl so angrily that he wondered whether he was grinding his teeth. 'He said, if you rangers were doing your job it wouldn't happen, would it?' The hide of the man. He trashes the environment and then blames us for not preventing it. I felt like throttling him.'

The reason for the fuss about the swan's egg was quite clear now. It wasn't Mitch that his father was shouting at. It was really Hardy Blight.

Thirteen

Although his mother kept his nose in his school-books during the week Mitch still had time to go fishing during the weekend. Sometimes he went over to the ocean beach early on Saturday morning to collect a bag of fresh cockles for bait, and then spent the rest of the time trying to build up a good supply of fish because the pelicans were hungrier than ever as they grew older.

One morning when he was returning over the sandhills he heard strange noises. He stopped and listened carefully, trying to calm his panting breath. It didn't take long to realise that the sounds were being made by human beings — rough voices, bursts of laughter, the clash of bottles being thrown down together. They were coming from a spot beyond a small sandhill on the left.

'Campers,' Mitch thought to himself. 'Picnickers.'

He crouched low and crept up towards the crest of the sandhill. By the time he reached the top he was down on his stomach, crawling like a lizard. Then, slowly and carefully he raised himself on his hands and peered down into the hollow below. He was right. Three or four men were lazing around the embers of a campfire, laughing and joking as they drank beer from a carton of stubbies. A couple of dune buggies were standing a few metres away.

Mitch guessed that the campers had been carousing there all night. He recognised two of them straight away — Hardy Blight and Jimmy Small. It was also clear that they would leave an awful mess behind them when they left because they would never dream of cleaning up their own rubbish.

Mitch sank down out of sight and lay on his stomach. A dozen thoughts raced about in his mind. As soon as he arrived back home he would tell his father about them — as he always did — and his father would want them to be prosecuted. But if they were brought before the court there would have to be a reliable witness. And who would that be but Mitchell Bird? It would be an awful ordeal for him, and the campers would despise him for the rest of their lives.

On the other hand, if he kept quiet about it the campers would never know they had been seen and he would never have to be a witness in court. But that would be like acting a lie. He would feel guilty for the rest of his life, and if his father and mother found out about it they would be ashamed of him. There was only one thing to do. He had to go home and tell them straight away.

He stood up, bending low and treading carefully, but his feet disturbed some of the loose sand at the the top of the sandhill and sent it streaming down in an avalanche. Several of the men looked up sharply and caught sight of him before he could sneak away. One of them jumped to his feet, the big man with a beard. Hardy Blight.

'Hey, you,' he yelled.

Mitch froze, unsure whether to run or stay.

'Whatya up to?'

Mitch decided to stand and face him. He was sure he could outrun all of them if they set off after him. He had the advantage of his position up on the sandhill and they were probably half drunk, flabby and unfit. They would be exhausted before they had climbed halfway up towards him, especially with their feet slipping backwards at every step. On the other they had their dune buggies beside them and they might try to run him down before he could reach his boat and escape across the Coorong.

'Whatya up to?' Hardy Blight yelled again.

'Nothing.'

'Snoopin', ya little runt?'

'I didn't even know you were here.'

'Whatya doin' over this side?'

'Getting cockles for bait.'

A light seemed to dawn in Hardy Blight's

head. He turned to his mates. 'Hey, it's the ranger's kid.'

The others got to their feet and stared up at Mitch. 'That mongrel,' one of them said.

'Come down here,' Hardy Blight called. 'We want to talk to ya.'

'You come up here,' Mitch answered cheekily. Hardy Blight took a step towards his buggy and Mitch's heart leaped. Without waiting he turned and fled, listening for the roar of the engines. There was no sound. After a hundred metres or so he slowed down, confident that the men had decided not to follow him. He hurried to his dinghy and headed for home as quickly as he could. Although he had escaped easily enough he was worried. The peninsula could be a dangerous place when you were on your own over there. In future he would have to be careful.

When he arrived home his father was away at a meeting and his mother was in the workshop. He hastened out to tell her about his clash with the campers.

She was alarmed at what could have happened. 'Keep away from them,' she said. 'Your father is having quite enough trouble with people like that. I don't want you to get involved as well.'

Mitch protested. 'But I didn't even know they were there. I just stumbled across them.'

'You went to look, didn't you? You could have gone past without anyone knowing about it.'

'But Dad's always saying that we *ought* to know about it. That's the only way we'll ever catch them.'

His mother sighed. 'Yes, yes, I've heard all that before. And I guess it would be useful if you were ever asked to give evidence.'

'That's why I'm going to write everything down — the date, the place where they had their campfire, how many there were, what they were doing, what they said to me …'

'Oh, so it's private detective Mitchell Bird, is it?' she said, smiling and tousling his hair. Then she turned and beckoned him to follow. 'Come with me. I've got something to show you.' She led the way inside to the special lamp-powered bird incubator and drew aside the little rug on the platform. 'Look.'

Mitch stared. Something tiny was lying there, something that was squirming about helplessly. 'It's hatched,' he cried. 'The swan's egg has hatched.'

She smiled broadly. 'Yes. You and your lamp have produced a tiny swan. More correctly, a tiny cygnet.'

Mitch peered closely. 'It's not very pretty, is it?'

'No, it's downright ugly. But that'll change. You know the story of the ugly duckling.'

'Yes.'

'Except that this ugly duckling won't turn into a snow white swan. It will be black, jet black, but very beautiful all the same.'

Mitch was overjoyed. 'If we hadn't hatched it the egg would have been left to rot, or the gulls would have eaten it.'

'I guess. But remember that you still have to make sure it survives. You'll have to keep it warm and feed it carefully.'

'It's terribly small.'

'Tiny. A ball of nothing with a neck.'

'But I'll look after it.'

'You're going to be busy, with the pelicans to feed as well. And all your schoolwork to do.'

Mitch wrinkled his nose. Plenty Full and Plenty Empty were growing at such a rate that it was hard to keep up their supply of fish. 'They're always hungry,' he complained. 'Both of them.'

'Your father warned you.'

'Yes, and he's going to rub it in forever.'

'The swan will be easier to feed. Greens and a bit of grain. And when it grows up it will be able to find widgeon grass for itself.'

Mitch looked at the tiny cygnet again. 'What are we going to call it?'

'You'll have to think of something. And let's not have any more nonsense names. How about a word that describes something special about swans.'

'Like what?'

'Colours? Black body, red beak, white flight feathers. Something like that.'

Mitch began to get the idea. 'Long necks?'

'Maybe their call.'

'Honking?'

'Yes. Or their call when they're flying over the

Coorong — that lovely fluting, sound. Like a sort of bugle.'

Mitch brightened. 'That's it. That's a beaut name.'

'What is?'

'Bugle.'

'Yes, it's fitting for a swan. Beautiful.'

So that was settled. Mitch now had three 'responsibilities' to care for every day — Plenty Full, Plenty Empty and Bugle.

Early next morning Mitch hurried to see whether little Bugle was still safe in his snug nest above the lamp. Happily he was very much alive, squirming about and wanting breakfast. Mitch's mother came over as well and they fed Bugle with tiny tidbits. 'He needs small bits every now and then,' she said, 'not one great dollop in the morning.'

Mitch appealed to her. 'Could you do it just for today, Mum? Please? I have to go fishing. If I don't catch lots of fish this morning I won't have enough to last Plenty Full and Plenty Empty through the week.'

His father who had been answering the phone in the next room came hurrying out with a bundle of papers in his hand. 'What did I say about pelicans being a burden?'

Mitch defended himself. 'But I did save them, Dad. All three of them. That's what we're supposed to be doing.'

His father put up his hand. 'OK. OK. But you'll only have yourself to blame if it's more than you can handle.'

Mitch gave him a wicked smile. 'Then you'll help me, won't you, Dad?'

His father snorted and started to walk away.

'You'd better come and have breakfast or you won't have time to catch anything,' his mother called. At the same moment there was a snackering sound outside. 'Plenty Full is knocking at the door,' she added. 'He says he's hungry.'

'He's always hungry,' Mitch grumbled. 'He'd gobble up a whole barrow load of fish if you let him. His name ought to be Never Full.'

Even his father laughed at that. 'You're learning fast,' he called over his shoulder. But there was a kind note in his voice that made Mitch feel better.

Although he would never have admitted it, he began to see that his father was right about the pelicans. They were already causing an enormous amount of work. It was never-ending. They had to be attended to every day and they needed an endless supply of food. And now he had Bugle to cope with as well. He would have to fence off part of the garden with birdwire to grow lettuces and other greens for him. There would be another roosting spot to wash out and scrub and clean. And on top of all that, if his schoolwork wasn't up to date Mrs Penn and his mother would want to know why.

He decided that there was something wrong with the stars in his horoscope that day because when he managed to get away in his boat at last the fishing was hopeless. He moved from place to place but the fish always seemed to be somewhere else. An hour went by, two hours, three hours, and still no fish. He didn't know what to do. The pelicans had to be fed, no matter what. If he couldn't catch food for them he would have to get it somewhere else. But where? The fish market? The cannery? A seafood shop? And who was going to pay for it? He could imagine the look on his father's face if he asked him for money to feed two pelicans he hadn't wanted in the first place.

Mitch started the outboard for the tenth time and went further up the Coorong. After a kilometre or two another boat came sailing within a few hundred metres of him, heading for a small wooden jetty on the shore. A building that looked more like a shack than a house was partly hidden in the scrub behind it.

Mitch recognised the boatman at once. It was Whiskers Burns, a strange old fisherman who had lived in the shack as long as anyone could remember. He kept to himself, and people told stories about him that weren't true. He had an enormous ginger beard that glowed in the afternoon light as though it really was on fire. Everyone joked about it. 'How did Whiskers Burns get his name?' they would say. 'Because he lit a match and proved that whiskers do.'

As Mitch neared the other boat he slowed down and edged forward gently until they were within a few metres of one another. He leaned forward and called. 'Hullo Mr …' He was on the brink of saying 'Mr Whiskers' but corrected himself in time. 'Mr … er Burns.'

The old man sat silently for a moment before answering. 'G'day, boy.'

Mitch was keen to be friendly. 'Good catch?' He could see that there were plenty of fish in the boat.

Whiskers looked down at them casually. 'Middling.'

'Better than me. Too much water between the fish today.' It was a terrible old joke but he wanted to sound like a grown up.

'It happens.'

'But I have to keep going. I've got a couple of pelicans to feed.' He realised at once that he had made a blunder. If there was one kind of bird that Whiskers was likely to detest more than any other it was greedy pelicans that came robbing his catch, damaging his nets and wanting a handout.

'Pelicans,' Whiskers answered sharply. 'I'd like to strangle 'em.'

The old man peered at him. His huge beard was greying slightly at the edges, flecked with dull spots as though it really had been on fire, leaving dead embers and wisps of white smoke.

'They're protected,' Mitch said defensively. 'I saved them.'

Whiskers softened his tone. 'Yeah. Yeah. I guess it's your dad's job.'

'Yes.'

'Maybe it's better if you do feed 'em. Then they won't come round pestering me.'

Time was passing and Mich still hadn't caught anything. 'I'd better get going,' he said, 'or I'll have to buy the fish.'

'That'd cost you.'

Mitch nodded. 'I know.'

'You want a few?'

Mitch was amazed. The last thing he expected from Whiskers was an offer to sell him fish — for pelicans, of all creatures. 'How much?' he asked uncertainly.

'Half price. That's all I get from the buyers anyway. They're all crooks.'

Mitch didn't know what to say, unsure whether to accept the offer or not. It would cost him money, but at least he would have some fish to take home. As things stood he was likely to spend all day out in his boat and still finish up with nothing at all.

'Thanks,' he answered. 'Thanks very much.'

He was thinking feverishly. 'But I haven't got any money with me.'

'No matter. Pay later.'

Mitch felt that he should accept the offer, not only to make sure that his pelicans had something to eat but to strike up a kind of friendship with Whiskers, who knew more about fishing in the Coorong than anyone on earth and who could be very helpful in the years ahead. He even wondered whether Whiskers was thinking the same thing in reverse. It was also wise for fishermen to be friendly with the rangers.

'OK,' he said. 'That's very kind of you.'

Whiskers took a bucket and almost filled it with mullet. Then he brought his boat alongside and hoisted the bucket over into Mitch's dinghy.

'How much?' Mitch asked.

'Five dollars.'

'Five dollars?' It was so cheap that Mitch couldn't think of anything proper to say. 'Thanks very much,' he stammered. Then, as an after-thought, he added 'I'll bring the bucket back when I pay you.'

'No worries.'

'I'll do it as soon as I can.'

Whiskers held out his hand. 'Shake on it.' They both reached out over the sides of the boats and shook hands. Mitch remembered how his grandfather had often told him that people did business like that long ago. No documents, no signatures, no receipts, just a handshake. That sealed an agreement better than any lawyer's piece of paper. It was never broken.

'You trusted people in those days,' his grandfather had said. 'A promise was a promise.'

As Mitch shook hands he felt confident and happy. He had made a pact with Whiskers. He would make sure that he honoured the handshake.

On his way home he wondered whether he should tell his father and mother about the deal. If they asked him directly whether he had caught any fish he would have to tell the truth. He hated telling lies, not only because it was wrong but because someone always found out about it. On the other hand, if his mother said something like, 'Have you brought home any fish?' he could answer yes without really telling a lie, even though he would probably feel uncomfortable about it. It was what she called a white lie.

He finally decided that he would say nothing unless he was asked. His father was sure to explode if he found out that Mitch was spending money on fish for the pelicans. There was no point in creating a scene if it wasn't necessary.

He moored the dinghy at the landing in front of the house, upended the fish into a wet bag, and hurried inside to pack them in the freezer. Luckily there was nobody about. He went back quickly and hid the bucket so that no-one would ask where it had come from. As soon as he could he would take it back to Whiskers and pay him the money. That would wind up the whole deal nicely.

Time passed quickly. Before long it was the middle of the year and cold winds were blasting up from the Southern Ocean. It was hard to make regular fishing trips in weather like that, so Mitch some-times had to use bird food or leftover scraps of fish from the dinner table to help feed the pelicans.

All three birds were growing quickly. The

little cygnet was much stronger now but it was still far from beautiful. Although it was going to grow into a black swan it wasn't black at all, but a brown-grey colour with pale ends to the feathers. 'Bugle,' Mitch said. 'You're a really ugly bird.'

'Don't be impatient,' his mother answered. 'Some day he'll be one of the most beautiful birds in the world.'

On days when the weather was bad Mitch spent most of the time hunched over his school books. Even when he had finished all his assignments his mother urged him to do something extra. He did more Maths problems, read more novels, prepared more maps and graphs to go with his reports, and started to write stories of his own.

Sometimes when he found an item in his father's encyclopedia and then logged onto it on the Internet he was surprised to find that the facts were different. When he complained about it his mother smiled. 'Don't always accept everything you see in a book or on a web page,' she said. 'People who prepare these things don't know it all. Like everyone else they sometimes get it wrong. So you need to double-check it.' Mitch was astonished.

He had always thought that anything in a book was sure to be right.

Mrs Penn came down on a mid-year visit, bringing a swag of new work with her. She sat down with Mitch and his mother and spent most of the day going through it, checking the difficult parts and setting the deadlines for the rest of the year. Mitch liked her more and more. He enjoyed her jokes and the clear way she explained things. But when she asked him whether he would prefer to be in a class at school instead of working on his own at home he hesitated. He liked the freedom he had to do things at his own pace and arrange his day in whatever way he liked, but he didn't want her to think he was a hermit or a misfit. And he knew that in eighteen months' time he would have to sit in a classroom again when he started high school in the city. It might be hard to get used to it.

'Are you ever lonely?' Mrs Penn asked.

'No. I'm happy here.'

'Not even a little bit?'

'No.'

'He's too busy,' Meg said. 'He hasn't any time

to be lonely. If he's not working at his books he's out on the Coorong in his boat.'

Mrs Penn smiled. 'Perhaps that's where he gets all the good ideas for the stories he writes.'

After lunch they stood on the verandah for a while and looked out over the water to the distant sandhills. Mrs Penn took a deep breath as if trying to draw it all in. 'I think I could stand here and look at it forever.'

Mitch's mother laughed. 'You mightn't always think so. Not when the south wind cuts like a knife.'

Mrs Penn spread her arms wide, as if trying to hold the whole Coorong in a hug. 'Surely a place like this is always beautiful. I can't imagine that it would ever be different.' She was so preoccupied that she was unaware that Plenty Full, Plenty Empty and little Bugle had come waddling along the verandah until she heard strange noises behind her. She turned quickly and and stepped back in amazement.

'Pelicans!'

'They're my pets,' Mitch said. 'I saved them.'

'And a little cygnet too.'

'He's the tamest of all.'

'Really?'

'Yes. We hatched him with a lamp.'

'With a *lamp*?'

Mitch's mother chuckled. 'We improvised an incubator. That's probably why he's so tame. He heard Mitch's voice every day while he was still in the egg. He thinks Mitch is his mother.'

Mrs Penn stared. 'And have you given him a name?'

'Yes, Bugle. His call will sound a bit like that when he grows up.'

'Into a black swan?'

'Yes.'

She turned to the two pelicans waiting expectantly near Mitch. 'And what about these two gentlemen?'

'I saved them when they were tiny babies. They're almost half grown now.'

'And you've given them names too?'

'Yes. They're Plenty Full and Plenty Empty.'

Mrs Penn rollicked with laughter. 'Which one is which?'

'The big one is Plenty Full. One day I said the

fish were plentiful, and dad said the pelican was plenty full too. That's how he got his name. He's always been bigger than Plenty Empty.'

Mrs Penn laughed so much that she had to dry her eyes. 'Mitchell,' she said at last, 'I can see why you don't miss your friends at school. Your brothers and sisters are pelicans, swans and all the other birds of the Coorong.'

During the following week Fos had to go up to the city to give evidence in a case against Hardy Blight and Jimmy Small. The police had finally charged them with driving in prohibited places, injuring wildlife, and damaging the environment. There were several other witnesses, all hoping that Hardy Blight had been caught at last. Meg agreed to stay at home and feed the birds so that Mitch could travel with his father because it would be a good experience for him. He rarely had a chance to visit the city.

Unfortunately the trial was a fiasco. Hardy was defended by a smart lawyer who browbeat the witnesses with so many questions that they became confused. 'The defendant was wearing dark glasses and a helmet when you say you saw him in his vehicle,' he said. 'How can you be sure that it wasn't someone else?' And when two people said they recognised Hardy because of his beard the lawyer produced five large photographs of men with beards who were wearing helmets and goggles. 'One of these men is the accused,' he said, and then asked each witness to identify him. Of course they could not.

The judge questioned whether the photographs were genuine but the lawyer said he had arranged a line-up of the men themselves and the witnesses could try to identify Hardy among them if they wished. Everyone knew it would be impossible. When Mitch's father was called to give evidence he pointed out various items that proved the case — an empty beer carton found among the litter in the National Park with H. Blight scrawled on it by someone at the hotel where Hardy had bought it, and photos of tyre prints in the sand near the campfire that appeared to match those on Hardy's dune buggy.

However the lawyer argued that anyone could

have dumped the carton where it was found. There were three or four H. Blights in the state, any one of whom could have been involved. And the impressions of the tyres were blurred because the loose sand had moved, especially at the edges of the grooves, making it doubtful whether they had really been made by Hardy's buggy. In any case, there were dozens of other buggies that used the same kinds of tyres.

In the end the judge dismissed the case. There wasn't enough evidence to prove it, and it would be unjust to convict two men who might be innocent. It was a maddening outcome. Everyone knew that Blight and Small were guilty but, as happens so often in court cases, there wasn't enough evidence to prove it.

Mitch's father was fuming when they came out of the court room. 'Corrupt lawyers,' he growled. 'They ought to be brought before the court themselves. By letting fellows like Blight off the hook they do as much damage to the environment as the vandals themselves. Now Blight can laugh in our faces and go on despoiling the place. And we can't do a thing to stop it.'

Mitch was angry too, more for his father's sake than his own.

That was not the end of the matter. An hour or so later when they went back to the side street where they had parked the Land Cruiser they found that both rear tyres were punctured. At first Mr Bird thought he must have run over a patch of broken glass or scattered nails of some kind, but when he looked more closely he drew in his breath and straightened up, white with anger. Both tyres had been slashed with a knife.

It had obviously been done by someone with a grudge soon after the court case had ended. The Land Cruiser would have been easy to spot, with the wildlife logo on the driver's door and RANGER in big letters on the roof above the windscreen. 'So,' Mitch's father said, pursing his lips. 'Now we have a vendetta on our hands.' Mitch didn't know what a vendetta was but it sounded ugly and unpleasant.

By the time they had reported the attack to the police and the head office of the wildlife department, it was late in the day. They had to arrange for two new tyres to be fitted to the Land Cruiser and for the old ones to be kept as evidence. The man from the tyre company was laconic. 'Somebody doesn't like you,' he said. 'In fact he doesn't like you at all.'

'Someone is a criminal,' Mr Bird answered savagely.

'No idea who did it?'

'I know who did it all right but I can't damn well prove it.'

'Rotten thing to do, two good tyres like that.'

'Yes.'

'Bad luck.'

'Not bad luck. Bad blood.'

'You'll have to watch out from now on.'

'From now on I'll have eyes in the back of my head.'

Mitch realised he would have to keep his own eyes open as well.

When they arrived home late that night his father was still seething. It was after ten o'clock before they could sit down to have something to eat.

'I've never been so frustrated in my life,' Fos said. 'Or so angry. Now Mr Smart Blight will think he can do whatever he likes, and snap his fingers at us while he's doing it. What's the point in saying that ninety-nine percent of the visitors to the Park are good people who never do any damage, when the other one percent is made up of oafs like Blight. He does more harm than all the others put together.'

'What's an oaf?' Mitch asked.

'A lout. A big stupid dolt,' his mother answered.

Fos laughed grimly. 'That describes Hardy Blight perfectly. He's true to his name — a real blight.'

Meg looked at Mitch quizzically. 'And what's a blight, Mitch?'

'Don't know.'

'It's a disease, a fungus, an infection that makes everything sick.'

'Exactly.' Mitch's father stood up and went off to bed. 'Including me,' he said as he left the room.

In late winter and early spring there were important changes in the Coorong. Between July and September the small crabs that lived in the rocky stretches along the mainland shore lost their shells. They were called 'softies' for a while until new hard shells grew back again, and so for a couple of months they were easy pickings for the big mulloway that came in from the open sea through the Murray Mouth. They were big fish, a metre long, weighing ten or twenty kilograms — sometimes even more — and they were as hungry as hunters. They feasted furiously on the crabs and on schools of mullet, biting into them viciously, smacking the water loudly like someone slapping the surface with the flat side of a paddle.

Mitch was not really interested in the mulloway, although they would have provided a wonderful feast for the pelicans when cut into pieces. They were too big for him to handle on his own. In any case, he didn't have the proper gear for them. There were also bream in sheltered spots along the shore, especially where tea trees grew near the edge of the water, but they were hard to catch. Mitch preferred to concentrate on the yellow-eye mullet. There were usually lots of them about and they were nice and manageable. When Mitch brought a good catch home the pelicans gobbled them so eagerly that he had to be careful they didn't swallow his hand as well.

Plenty Full and Plenty Empty were big birds now, although they didn't yet have their full flight feathers. They plodded about in the yard and on the front verandah, looking out at the Coorong keenly as though some strong instinct kept calling them down to the water. Mitch wondered whether they would leave him as soon as they could fly.

Bugle was even tamer than the pelicans. He followed Mitch everywhere, even into the house if the door was open, poking about inside as though it was the natural thing to do. Whenever Mitch decided to go fishing Bugle followed him down to the boat and was plainly broken-hearted if he thought Mitch was preparing to sail away without him. He made little crooning noises as if crying because he couldn't swim fast enough to keep up with the boat, and couldn't follow in the air because he wasn't old enough to fly.

One day, as Mitch was about to push off he looked down at Bugle at the edge of the water. 'OK,' he said impulsively 'Today, you can come too.' And he lifted him up and stood him at the bow of the boat. Bugle seemed so happy that Mitch had a lump in his throat at the sight of him.

That was the beginning of their great friendship. They were inseparable. Wherever Mitch went Bugle went too, whether it was a simple trip to get a spanner from the shed or a carrot from the garden. And whenever he decided to go down to the boat Bugle seemed to read his mind and hurried off ahead of him so quickly that he was waiting on the landing before Mitch reached it.

Before long people began to talk about it. 'Have you seen the boy in the boat with the little swan?' they asked.

'Yes, the ranger's kid.'

'Follows him everywhere.'

'Won't leave his side. Never seen anything like it.'

'Hard to believe.'

'Just like the story of the Snow Goose — you know, the one that followed its master to the war.'

'Don't know that story but I reckon it's the sort of thing this bird would do.'

'Incredible.'

After working hard during the week Mitch always looked forward eagerly to the week-end when he was free to do what he liked. Apart from cleaning the garden shed where Plenty Full and Plenty Empty roosted each night, and doing the same to the corner of the workshop that was Bugle's home, he could use most of the time to build up his fish supply or create startling inventions of his own. He therefore had time on his hands one Saturday when his father called him after breakfast and said, 'I have to run up to the Point today to check on a few things. Want to come?'

Mitch was always pleased when his father invited him on a trip like that. It made him feel that he was being treated like a grown-up.

'Sure,' he answered. 'When do we leave?'

'As soon as we can.'

'I'll get ready straight away.'

'Get your hat and water bottle. Sun glasses too.'

'Right.' Mitch hesitated. 'What about Bugle? Can he come too?'

His father muttered impatiently because he didn't particularly want to be seen with a bird in his boat.

'Must you?'

'He won't be any trouble, Dad. He always comes with me.'

His father grumbled but finally agreed. 'Well, all right, if you must.'

They set off and made good time. His father's Government boat was so much bigger than Mitch's dinghy that Bugle was able to sit on the roof of the wheelhouse, craning forwards with his long neck like the figurehead on the fast sailing clippers of long ago.

They were nearing the Point when a fishing boat came sailing towards them. Mitch recognised it at once — Whiskers Burns on his way home after a night's fishing. As the two boats approached each other they slowed to a stop while the men exchanged greetings. Mitch could see that Whiskers had made a big haul of mulloway. Mr Bird pointed at them. 'Good catch.'

Whiskers was standing at the wheel with a stranger beside him. Mitch knew that it would have been impossible to make a catch of big fish like that without someone to help him.

'Yeah,' he called back. 'Would you like one?'

Mitch's father was surprised by the offer. 'That's very generous of you.'

'Don't mind sharing.'

Mitch knew that mulloway were tasty because his mother sometimes grilled a few pieces. They were scrumptious. Perhaps that was why many people called them butterfish.

'It's very kind of you to offer, but no. Thanks all the same.'

'That's OK. Just like to be neighbourly.' Whiskers looked so directly at Mitch when he said it that Mitch was terrified he was going to mention their deal with the bucket of mullet. He had never told his mother and father about it and felt guilty that he hadn't.

'See you then,' Whiskers called as he opened the throttle and moved away. He lifted his hand in a friendly farewell and pointed at Bugle. 'Fine bird you've got there.

'Bye. Thanks again.'

Mitch was disappointed that his father had

refused the offer. 'It would have been nice, that mulloway,' he said.

'Yes, it would.'

'Why didn't you take it, then?'

His father looked at him calmly. 'I couldn't afford to, Mitch.'

'What do you mean? Did you think he was going to charge too much for it?'

'No, no. He wasn't going to charge anything at all.'

'Well then?'

'That's just the problem.'

'Why.'

'It would have compromised me. Do you know what that means?

'No.'

'I would have owed him a favour. People who heard about it would accuse me of accepting bribes.'

'I don't get it.'

'Say, for instance, I caught Whiskers doing something illegal one day. He might expect me to overlook it because he had given me the fish — ask me to turn a blind eye.'

'But Whiskers wouldn't do a thing like that. He's a good bloke.'

'Of course he is. But I can't afford to owe a favour to anyone. Not ever. Can you imagine what someone like Hardy Blight would do if he found out about it? He'd spread stories. He'd exaggerate and distort it. Before long he'd start to convince people that I was doing illegal deals in secret. And once stories like that get around it's very hard to undo the damage no matter how innocent you are or how hard you try to prove that they're not true.'

Mitch was shocked. He went up and sat with Bugle for the rest of the trip. The world, he decided, could sometimes be a crazy place.

Time seemed to pass more quickly as the year went on. Before long the last term had started and Mitch was busier than ever. Mrs Penn often called him to explain new questions or correct any of his answers that were wrong. Projects and assignments kept piling up and his mother pushed him hard to get them done.

Meanwhile his three 'responsibilities' were

growing up quickly. Plenty Full and Plenty Empty could fly. They sometimes took off and disappeared down the Coorong for a while but they always came back to be fed. 'You'd think they could catch a few fish for themselves by now,' Mitch grumbled, 'instead of depending on me all the time.'

His father opened his mouth as if about to say 'I told you so' but decided against it. 'They've never had a father or mother to teach them,' he said. 'You saved their lives, but if you turned them out into the wild now I doubt whether they would survive.'

When his father spoke like that Mitch felt guilty. Perhaps he shouldn't have rescued the baby pelicans after all. On the other hand he knew that he couldn't have walked away and left them to die. They would have haunted his mind for the rest of his life, lying there helplessly while they gasped their lives away. So now it was his job to look after them. He was determined to do that, no matter what.

When they were flying effortlessly overhead, or when they came gliding down onto the water, they were beautiful to watch, but when they sat side by side on the land they looked like pudgy professors discussing the difficulties of the world. 'Good morning, gentlemen,' Mitch's mother often said when she opened the door in the morning. 'What problems are we solving today?'

'How to get more fish,' Mitch answered. 'They never think of anything else.'

He eyed Plenty Full, who seemed to be getting plumper every day. 'Why don't you get some exercise, you big fat lump? Fly over to the beach for a day.'

Meg laughed. 'He'll do that easily enough — when he's in the mood.'

Bugle was very different. He was trim and elegant and already very beautiful with his proud head and arched neck. Because he was young his body feathers were still dull grey instead of deep black, and the flight feathers on his wings were not yet bright white. But when he rose into the air he looked like a jet with his wings curved back and his head and neck thrust forward. Even Mitch's father admired him. 'Yes,' he said, 'he's growing into a really beautiful swan.'

'How do you know whether he's a boy or a girl?' Mitch asked.

'The male's bill is longer and straighter. And he's bigger than the female.'

'I'm glad he's so tame.'

'Yes he is. But you may have to be careful when he's fully grown. He'll hiss and attack like fury when he's angry.'

'He wouldn't do that to me. I'm his friend.'

'Let's hope it stays that way.'

Fourteen

$\mathcal{T}$he last term ended with a rush. Almost before he was aware of it Mrs Penn was writing to congratulate him on his good final report. 'Mitchell has been an excellent student,' she wrote. 'We look forward to working with him again next year.'

In less than two weeks they were celebrating Christmas. Mitch's uncle and aunt, Harry and Nancy Bird, came down from the city and stayed until the new year. They all had a great time together, sometimes fishing, sometimes cruising about on the Coorong, and sometimes just lounging on the front verandah and admiring the view.

'What a life,' Uncle Harry said jokingly. 'Nothing to do and all day to do it.'

Mitch's father growled. 'You can take over if you like, especially at this time of the year.'

Mitch knew what his father was referring to. During the holidays many more people visited the National Park and caused problems. Some came from towns further down the coast and roared up the beach on trail bikes and jalopies; some screamed about on the water in jet skis terrifying the birds and upsetting other holiday makers; some camped in the scrub or picnicked on the shore and left litter everywhere. There were constant telephone calls from people complaining about other people.

'Trouble?' Uncle Harry asked one day when the phone kept ringing.

Mitch's father was fair. 'Not always. Many callers just want a bit of advice about rules in the Park. They're sensible and caring, and sometimes even help us by cleaning up someone else's mess.

We don't want to stop good people like that from enjoying the place.'

'But some are not like that?'

'A few are a pain in the butt.'

'Like who?'

'There's a guy called Hardy Blight and his off-sider Jimmy Small. They cause more trouble than all the others put together.'

'What do they do?'

'What don't they do! For instance the beach down beyond the Murray Mouth is closed between October and December so that the birds can breed safely. But Blight ignores rules like that and roars about regardless.'

'In a buggy?'

'You could call it that. He even pollutes the air because he never maintains the engine properly. The last time I saw him it was pouring out more smoke than a factory chimney. That's the sort of dolt he is.'

Just then the telephone rang again and Mitch's father went off to answer it. When he came back he was shaking his head. 'You wouldn't believe it,' he said. 'Someone has been stealing petrol and fishing gear from the boats while they're tied up for the holidays.'

Uncle Harry was disgusted. 'Is that how thieves celebrate Christmas?'

As they were talking, Bugle came walking along the verandah to join them.

'Here comes Larry Long Neck,' Uncle Harry joked. 'Plod, plod, plod.'

Mitch's mother protested. 'He's not a plodder. Anything but.'

'He walks like a scuba diver with his flippers on.'

'He's not built to walk on land, but just watch him on the water or in the air.'

Uncle Harry looked at Bugle closely. 'Bugle,' he said. 'You've got the most incredible neck. It's longer than your body.'

'That's how it's meant to be,' Mitch's father said. 'He can do almost anything with it — preen his chest, clean his wings, even scratch the back of his neck.'

'It's as flexible as rubber. I wish I could twist my neck about like that. I'd be able to look around corners.'

'You could if you had twenty joints in it like Bugle. Twenty vertebrae, that is.'

'Like a giraffe?'

'No, no, no. A giraffe only has seven. Bugle has three times as many.'

'So he arches it and swivels it about all the time?'

'On land, yes. But in the air his head and neck point straight ahead like a missile.'

'Yes, I've seen them.'

'Very beautiful really.'

Meanwhile Bugle had settled down quietly beside Mitch, tucked his head under his wing, and gone to sleep. He was not interested in discussions about the length of his neck.

<hr />

Mitch had the whole of January to himself. He loved the freedom of it. Apart from keeping an eye on the garden he had the rest of the time to create more weird inventions in the workshop or build up a good supply of fish in the freezer. Now and then he watched a video or played a computer game but he preferred life outside. Most of the time he was out in the sun with a wide hat on his head and a light shirt on his back to prevent his skin from roasting.

Whenever he went out fishing Plenty Full, Plenty Empty and Bugle went with him. Bugle sat motionless in his favourite spot in the bow of the boat but the two pelicans often took off and circled overhead like a couple of lumbering planes keeping watch on the world below. When they saw him catch a fish they came back to the boat in a flash and eyed the catch greedily. Mitch had to be careful that they didn't try to snatch it away and swallow the hook as well, but they seemed to have learnt that this was forbidden. At the end of the day he gave each of them a fish for being good.

One day in the middle of January Mitch accidentally let the boat drift into shallow water near the shore. Suddenly Bugle sprang down, upended himself, and probed about in the muddy bottom with his beak. Mitch was delighted.

'Good boy, Bugle,' he called when the swan came up again. 'You've learnt to feed yourself.'

He was so pleased that he waited for an hour or more while Bugle fed on the roots and tubers of the widgeon grass. He wondered what instinct had shown him how to do it, without a mother or father to teach him. He was also afraid that Bugle might decide to leave him now and go off to live his own life on the Coorong, but he need not have worried. When he had eaten enough Bugle swam back gracefully, flew up onto the boat, and settled down in his favourite position.

Fifteen

A few days later Mrs Bird came into the kitchen carrying a bucketful of tomatoes. They were beautiful — big, firm and rosy red. 'Your garden is too successful,' she said. There are enough greens out there to feed a whole flock of swans, and now the tomatoes are bearing too.' She hoisted the bucket onto the kitchen bench. 'There are far too many for us to use. We'll have to give some away.'

On the spur of the moment Mitch had an idea. 'Why don't I take some up to old Whiskers Burns? Nobody ever gives him anything.'

His mother hesitated. 'I'm not sure you should be seeing someone like that. We don't really know him, do we?'

'I know him. I've … I've …' Mitch almost let slip the story of his secret deal with Whiskers but checked himself just in time. 'I've met him out in the boat. So has Dad,' he added quickly.

His mother was still unhappy about the idea but in the end she agreed. 'All right, I'll pack a dozen in a box. Be careful not to drop them.'

'I'll ride up the road on my bike. It'll take forever if I go in the boat.'

Mitch's mother was not happy about that idea either. 'Be careful on the road.'

'Sure.'

'There are lunatic drivers out there who think they're Formula One champions. Keep well over to the side of the road.'

'Sure, Mum.'

It was hot on the highway and his mother was right about the traffic. Cars and trucks flashed by endlessly like competitors on a raceway. Sometimes the wind of their speed was so great that he almost lost his balance. Halfway along he passed the local roadhouse and petrol station and he was tempted to stop for a drink, but decided against it because he had promised his mother he would be as quick as he could. The man who ran the petrol station was Wally Eels and his name and initials — W H EELS — were printed in large letters above the workshop. Naturally, everyone called him Wheelie.

Mitch was tired and thirsty by the time he reached the track that wound down to the shack where Whiskers lived. He was afraid the old man might be away in his boat, but he need not have worried. He had barely knocked when Whiskers appeared in the doorway, peering at him out of his enormous beard. He was the hairiest man Mitch had ever seen.

'G'day, boy,' he said in his gravelly voice.

'I … I've brought you some tomatoes.' Mitch said hastily. 'We've got more than we need. And a lettuce too, and some greens. I grow them for my swan.' Mitch's heart was beating so fast and he had to hurry to get the words out in short bursts between each breath. He took the box of tomatoes and held it forward.

Whiskers was surprised for a moment but then a smile appeared out of his beard and he took them gratefully. 'That's very kind of you, boy. I owe you.'

'No, you did me a favour, remember? With the fish.'

'Should've given 'em to you.'

They both paused, facing each other in the doorway.

'Rode up on your bike?' Whiskers asked.

'Yes.'

'Hot work. Specially today. The old man turned and beckoned Mitch inside. 'Come on in. Get y' a drink. Bet you're as dry as a gibber.'

'Thanks. Thanks very much.'

Whiskers rummaged about in his fridge. 'Coke?'

'Coke would be fine.'

'Might have one myself.'

Whiskers pushed aside an untidy clutter on the kitchen table — two half-empty tins of jam, a sauce bottle, unwashed cups and plates, stubbies, old newspapers, letters and bits of mail — and they sat together silently, holding their drinks like a couple of old mates. Mitch felt uncomfortable because he couldn't think of anything to say. The silence went on and on until, quite suddenly, Whiskers turned to him and said 'Someone's bin swipin' petrol from outa the boats.' He looked at Mitch sharply.

'Yes,' he stammered. 'Dad's heard about it.'

'Lousy thing to do.'

'Yes.'

'Skunks, they are. Specially at Christmas.'

'Yes.' Repeating 'yes' all the time sounded dumb but Mitch couldn't think of anything else.

'Did they take some of yours too?' he managed at last.

'Not mine. They'd know I'm watchin'. Never go away.'

'Dad says it's hard for the police to find out who did it.'

Whiskers touched the side of his nose with his finger. 'You can sniff it out, I reckon. C'n always smell a rat.'

'Can you?'

Whiskers stood up and went over to the fridge to get two more cans of Coke.

'Y' hear things. Up and down. Round about.'

Mitch could see that Whiskers was talking in riddles because he didn't want to say what he knew. Perhaps he was afraid that if the thieves suspected him they would try to shut him up. He would be an easy target, alone and hidden in the scrub. It made Mitch uneasy. He finished his drink and said he had to go. At the door Whiskers thanked him again. 'Remember, boy,' he added, 'you c'n see things and hear things. Tell your dad. That'll sniff it out.'

As he rode away Mitch thought it sounded weird to be sniffing things out with his eyes and ears. He had no idea what he was supposed to tell his father, except that Whiskers seemed to know something about the petrol thieves but was unwilling to say much about it.

On his way home the highway was hotter than ever and the cars and trucks seemed to be racing more frantically. 'Why does everyone have to tear up and down like rats in a race all the time?' he grumbled to himself. 'What's the point of it?' When two big semi-trailers hurtled past him in quick succession the blast of wind they created sent him wobbling onto the gravel at the side of the road. He recovered just in time. He could imagine the blood on his knees and the gravel rash on his elbows if he'd gone skidding down the slope. 'I hate you,' he yelled after them but his voice was no more than the squeak of a mouse in a whirlwind.

There was worse to come. A few metres further on he heard a whistling hiss of air behind him and the back wheel started to bump along on its rim. A puncture. Flat back tyre. 'Bugger,' he growled. 'All because of those idiot trucks who pushed me into the gravel.' There was nothing he could do about the puncture so he trudged off down the hot strip of highway, wheeling the bike at his side. He could see Wheelie's petrol station in the distance, its outline rippling in the mirage. He hoped that he could reach it before he collapsed in the heat. He was glad it wasn't five kilometres away.

Wheelie had just finished pumping petrol for a couple of cars. He was standing beside his rusty old ute, which was parked against the roadhouse wall. A mobile set of shelves stood nearby, loaded with cans of oil, tins of grease, batteries, spare tyres and all kinds of odds and ends for motorists. He smiled as Mitch limped up, wet with perspiration.

'G'day, Mitch', he said. 'Bitzer let you down?'

Mitch was out of breath. 'Yeah,' he panted. 'Flat tyre.'

'Nail or something?'

'Sharp bit of gravel, I think.' He looked at Wheelie pleadingly. 'Could you fix it for me, Mr Eels? Please.'

Wheelie smiled. 'I reckon. Bring the bike around to the workshop.'

Mitch was amazed at the way Wheelie levered off the tyre and pulled out the tube in a couple of seconds. 'You're right,' he said. 'Something punched a hole through the wall of the tyre.' He pointed. 'Here, see?'

Mitch looked at it unhappily. 'Will it need a new tube?'

'Nah. I'll patch it. Only take a minute.'

Mitch was desperately thirsty. 'Do you think I could have a drink please, Mr Eels?' he asked.

'Sure. Take a can from the fridge in the shop.'

'But I haven't got any money with me.'

'That's OK. Pay me next time your dad comes by.'

Mitch was so grateful that he thanked Wheelie three times. 'You'll have to help yourself because my wife is away today,' Wheelie called after him. 'She usually runs the shop.'

Mitch had just gone inside when he heard the sound of engines pulling up beside the pumps — a deep-throated rumble that he recognised instantly. Dune buggies. He peered out through the door and then drew back hastily. Hardy Blight and Jimmy Small were sitting in their buggies with the engines still idling. A moment later they switched them off and the smoke from their exhausts hung about for a while like a dirty fog. Wheelie went over and started to fill their tanks without saying anything.

Mitch was in a panic. He desperately wanted to keep out of sight, hoping that Hardy and Jimmy would simply hand Wheelie the money for the petrol without getting out of their seats and then drive off. He was out of luck. After a minute or so Hardy eased himself out of his buggy, stretched hugely like a big black bear, and walked over to the roadhouse door. Jimmy followed, and so did Wheelie.

There were several fixtures about two metres high standing in the middle of the shop. They were loaded with magazines, bags of potato chips, chocolate bars, and all kinds of treats meant to tempt passing travellers. Two big fridges with glass doors stood against the far wall.

Mitch crouched behind the fixtures with his heart pounding, afraid that Hardy was going to come walking around them, picking and choosing from the racks. Luckily he only wanted something to drink. He and Jimmy went straight to the fridges, took out a couple of cans, and walked back to the counter to pay. Then they went outside, holding the cans to their mouths. Wheelie put the money for the drinks and the petrol in the till and went back to the workshop to fix the tyre.

From his hiding place behind the fixtures Mitch found it hard to see what was going on. The angle of his view through the glass of the entrance door only showed him an oblong patch of the world outside, and even that was partly blocked by the ute and display shelves. As they went out Hardy and Jimmy tossed their empty cans into the bin by the door. 'Well, well,' Mitch thought wryly. 'Today we're not throwing our rubbish about.'

After a few more steps they disappeared behind the mobile racks but Mitch still crouched in his hiding place, waiting for the sound of their engines. His knees were starting to ache. 'Come on, don't take all day,' he muttered. He craned forward, trying to see what they were doing. As he did so he glimpsed a pair of hands reaching out towards the shelves. They grabbed two five-litre cans of oil and disappeared in a blink. A moment later the engines started with a roar and he heard the buggies accelerating away down the highway. Mitch was thunderstruck. He ran outside and gazed after them but the buggies were already dwindling out of sight. Only the rumble of their engines remained.

His first impulse was to rush into the work- shop to warn Wheelie that he had just been robbed. But at the door he paused. All kinds of thoughts were racing about in his head. What could Wheelie do? What *would* he do? If he went straight to the police they would want proof. 'Any witnesses?' they would say. That's what it always came down to. And who was the only witness this time? Mitchell Bird. For some reason it always seemed to be Mitchell Bird.

What if Hardy Blight found out that Mitch had spied on him? He might want to shut him up. Even if he was arrested it would be his word against Mitch's. And he would have that smart, fox-faced lawyer to defend him again, overwhelming Mitch with trick questions.

By the time he walked into the workshop Mitch was tongue-tied. Once or twice he was on the point of telling Wheelie but he couldn't bring himself to do it. His bike was ready just as another traveller pulled up at the pumps and Wheelie hurried off to serve him. Mitch had lost his opportunity. All he could do was call 'thank you' and ride away.

By the time he arrived home he felt guilty and ashamed. He knew he had acted like a wimp. If everyone chickened out like that criminals would be able to get away with anything. As he parked his bike his father happened to come out to get something from the shed. Mitch went over to him uncertainly. 'Dad,' he said.

His father turned. 'Yes, son?'

Even at the last moment Mitch wanted to walk away, but it was too late. He blurted out his story in a rush and then stood waiting shame-facedly. Surprisingly, his father didn't shout at him. 'You should have told Mr Eels,' he said quietly, 'but I can understand why you hesitated.'

Mitch stood silently, waiting for his father to go on.

'You didn't want to be involved?'

Mitch shook his head. 'No.'

'Because you might have to be a witness?'

'Yes.'

'It was good of you to tell me, Mitch.'

He turned briskly and headed for the Land Cruiser. 'Come on,' he called. 'We'll go straight back. You can say what you saw and Mr Eels can call the police. If they move quickly they might be able to catch Hardy Blight with the oil still in the back of his buggy.'

Mitch followed miserably. More than any-thing else, he wanted to run away and hide.

The last few days of the holidays were slipping away quickly and the new school year was looming. Mitch was afraid that the police would arrive at any minute to interview him, and his heart skipped every time a car pulled up in the yard. But as the days went by calmly he began to breathe a little easier. He almost hoped that Wheelie and the police had decided to drop the whole thing, but that would mean that Hardy Blight would get away with the stolen oil and Mitch wasn't happy about that either.

He spent as much time as he could out in the boat. It helped him to forget about Wheelie's road-house and everything to do with it, and it gave him the chance to catch more fish. Plenty Full, Plenty Empty and Bugle went with him every day. Bugle as usual was in the bow with his long neck pointing the way. The two pelicans sat in the stern or the body of the boat, sometimes flying off for a while but always returning and always keenly interested in the fish Mitch managed to catch.

Many people were still enjoying their summer holidays and there were lots of boats on the water, most of them sailing about idly. Some were day trippers — tourists who had hired a boat or paid for a short cruise on the Coorong. One day a cabin cruiser came sailing down the channel towards the spot where Mitch was anchored. Plenty Full and Plenty Empty sat eyeing it calmly like a couple of VIPs who had learned to put up with nuisances of that kind. Bugle was more uncertain. He stood up and leaned forward as though about to take off and fly back to the house, but he settled down after a minute and became a living figurehead again.

The cabin cruiser was very expensive, with polished timber, shining paint and gleaming fittings. There were two men and three women on board, all looking expensive too. They gazed at Mitch and his three birds for a moment and then rushed to get their cameras. The skipper cut his engine to an idle and let the cruiser drift while they took their pictures.

'Hey,' one of the men called, 'are those birds for real?'

Mitch was uncomfortable at the way they were all gawking at him but he thought it best to answer politely.

'They're my friends.'

'Did it take long to tame them?'

'I didn't tame them. I saved them. They live with me.'

The man gurgled something that Mitch couldn't catch. A woman with a ridiculous hat on her head and jewellery that sparkled on her wrists and fingers leaned forward and pointed. Mitch couldn't understand why anyone would want to wear rings and bracelets out on the Coorong, but he knew that some people did weird things.

'Is that a cormorant?' she called. 'The bird in the front?'

Mitch stared at her in amazement. 'No,' he called back. 'It's a swan.'

'Oh. A swan?'

'Yes, a black swan. It's not really black yet because it's not quite fully grown.'

The skipper joined in the interchange across the water. 'Did you train them to come with you?'

Mitch was fed up. 'I didn't train them to do anything. They come with me because they want to.'

'Of their own free will?'

'Yes.'

'Incredible.'

He revved the engine and the cruiser edged away. Mitch pulled up his anchor and moved to another spot. 'What a load of dumb-brains,' he thought. 'All they do is waste other people's time. At this rate I'll never catch any fish.'

If he had known what the gawkers were saying later that day he would have been even more astonished. They were in the hotel at Goolwa, telling their story to everyone.

'You wouldn't believe it, this kid in a boat with three birds sitting beside him. They didn't fly off when we came up. Unreal.'

'One was a black swan,' the woman with the jewellery said. 'It wasn't a cormorant.' She turned to the skipper. 'What were the other two birds, Darren — the ones with the big beaks?'

'Pelicans.'

'Yes, pelicans.'

'We took pictures,' the skipper said. 'Can't wait to develop them.'

'Who is he?' one of the other men asked. 'The kid in the boat?'

The publican was pouring another round of drinks. 'That'd be the ranger's lad.'

'The ranger?'

'Yeah. Fos Bird. The boy's name is Mitch.'

The skipper spluttered in his beer. 'Bird? The ranger's name is Bird?'

'Yes.'

'You're joking.'

'No, dinkum.'

'I love it. I love it. Someone ought to send a film crew down there. It would make a good short.'

Unfortunately the skipper's words soon came true. He told the story so often that before long people began to ask where they could find the boy with the birds. Visitors turned up without notice, wanting to take photos. Tourist offices telephoned to see if they could print notices about Mitch in their brochures. Bus companies wanted to break their journeys in front of the house so that the passengers could see the 'Bird Boy'. Mitch was red with embarrassment, his mother was tired out and his father was livid.

'The place is a madhouse,' he stormed. He glared at Mitch. 'I knew there would be trouble when you got yourself involved with those birds, but I didn't dream it would ever come to this. It's a nightmare. People have gone crazy.'

'That's tourism,' Mitch's mother said. For once there was a touch of acid in her voice. 'Tourists are inquisitive. They want to see things. Unusual things.'

'Well they'll see something unusual if this goes on much longer. It'll be me, going out of my mind. You can guess what the other rangers are saying. They're laughing their heads off.'

Meg sighed. 'Maybe it will die down soon,' she said hopefully. 'Most of these things are just a flash in the pan.'

Poor Mitch just suffered in silence while all this was going on. He knew that he was to blame. He had caused the fuss by rearing the birds in the first place. If he ran away and lived in a cave the hullabaloo would end in a day.

Actually his mother put an end to it very simply. She told Mitch that she would buy fish for the pelicans each week so there would be no need for him to go out in the boat, at least for the time being. There was always food for Bugle in the garden, and if he wanted to he could fly out and get widgeon grass in the Coorong. In that way they could all stay at home. Any tourists who arrived would be told politely that there was nothing to see. And when the fuss had died down everyone could go back to a normal life. In any case, the new school year was about to start and Mitch would be too busy to go out fishing for a while.

His mother smiled at him. 'That's it,' she said. 'Problem solved.'

Mitch felt better already. He thought his mother was one of the smartest women in the world.

Mitch was delighted when he heard that Mrs Penn was going to be his Distance Education teacher again in the new year, because he had feared that he would be allotted to someone else. She came down as usual at the beginning of the term, bringing all the details of the year's work. Mitch and his mother spent most of the day with her, going through his program.

Although they worked hard they had time to have fun, especially after lunch. Mrs Penn had heard about the tourist fuss and had seen one or two items about it on television. She turned to Mitch. 'I hear that your birds are under arrest,' she joked. 'Or are they in quarantine?'

'They're happy to stay around the house,' Mitch answered. 'Sometimes they fly off but they always come back.'

'And I guess they always will?'

'Yes.'

'They're happy living here,' Mitch's mother said. Bugle loves playing games with Mitch. One of his favourites is Hunt-for-the-Treasure.'

Mrs Penn was curious. 'Show me. Is Bugle about?'

Mitch got up and looked out of the window. 'Yes, he's in his favourite spot on the verandah with his head tucked under his wing.'

He loves a sort of water radish that we grow in the garden, Mitch's mother said. 'It's very bland. It must taste a bit like the rhizomes of the widgeon grass. They're like tubers. You should see him if he knows that Mitch is trying to hide some of them.'

Mitch took four or five of the radishes and

kept them hidden in his hand while he walked out onto the verandah. His mother and Mrs Penn followed.

Bugle was wide awake as soon as he heard them coming. Mitch gave him a radish and slipped another one slyly into the pocket of his shirt. Bugle swallowed the first one in a flash and started to probe about eagerly for the second.

'How does he know it's in there?' Mrs Penn asked.

'They play the game so often that I guess he's learned all the tricks.'

Bugle soon showed that he had. No matter where Mitch hid the tidbits Bugle quickly winkled them out. His long neck curved and twisted in all kinds of impossible ways. Mrs Penn was delighted. 'It's like an elephant's trunk searching for peanuts, but more flexible.'

'Yes, it is.'

'Is he always so gentle?'

'He is with Mitch, but I doubt whether he would be so friendly with strangers. And if he and a pen ever bred some little cygnets, I wouldn't advise anyone to venture too close. Bugle would probably honk and hiss like fury. Even attack. Swans can be quite dangerous.'

'Did you say a "pen"?'

'Yes. The mother is a pen and the father is a cib.'

Mrs Penn was fascinated. 'Well, I didn't know that. So because I'm a Penn I'm also a female swan,' she joked. 'What a nice idea.'

Mitch ran inside just then and came out with a couple of fish for Plenty Full and Plenty Empty, who were standing eagerly nearby. 'If I give something to Bugle I always have to give something to these two as well,' Mitch said. 'Otherwise they get jealous and follow me around all the time with their beaks open.'

Mrs Penn chuckled. 'You could put on a little sideshow and charge everyone a dollar.'

Mitch's mother threw up her hands in horror. 'Heaven forbid! We've had enough of such circuses to last a lifetime.'

For a while things ran smoothly, except for a few days when Mitch had the flu. It was the first time

in his life that he had ever been sick in bed. His mother nursed him and then helped him catch up the work he had missed. His father was as busy as ever, but he found time now and then to take him out on a trip. They got on well together. After a while Mitch started fishing again but he wasn't pestered by camera-happy strangers. The tourist season had ended and the locals knew him so well that the sight of 'the boy, the birds, and the boat' as they said, was just part of normal life.

And then, quite suddenly, there was trouble again. Mitch and his father were at the roadhouse filling the tanks of the Land Cruiser with diesel when Wheelie came over.

'You wouldn't believe it,' he said. 'The gall of the fellow.'

'Who?' Mitch's father asked.

'Blight. Big-mouth Blight.'

Mitch's heart jumped and he felt weak.

'What happened?'

'He blew in here like a dust storm and accused me of spreading rumours abut him.'

'What rumours?'

'Stealing oil from me.'

'How did he get onto that?'

'Don't know. The police came and spoke to me a long time ago. Asked me whether I wanted to lay charges against Blight.'

'What did you say?'

'I said no. It would have cost me more than the oil was worth. But Blight must have got wind of it somehow. He reckons someone dobbed him in.'

Mitch stood still and listened in panic. 'Did … Did he know it was me?' he asked.

'He didn't say.'

Fos was angry. 'I like his front. Playing Mr Innocent.'

'He knows he can get away with it. That's what sticks in my throat.'

Mitch climbed back miserably into the Land Cruiser. He didn't want to be involved with Hardy Blight again. Not ever.

～∾ ∾～

Plenty Full and Plenty Empty were big birds now. When Plenty Full stood up proudly he looked like the king of the pelicans, and although Plenty Empty was still smaller than his brother, his name was no longer apt. Bugle was growing up steadily too. Mitch knew that swans grew fairly slowly but he could see that Bugle was going to be a big, beautiful bird. When he rose into the air his flight feathers stood out clear and white and his head and neck were thrust forward, longer than the main part of his body. His bill was almost bright red now, with the white band of a grown-up swan, and the feathers of his body were deepening into black. His eyes were black too, with a thin circle of white.

Mitch often picked him up in his arms and rubbed his cheek against Bugle's neck. 'You are the loveliest swan on the Coorong,' he said. 'You should be called Prince Bugle.'

His mother laughed at that, and even his father managed a smile. 'As long as he is free to come and go as he likes,' he said. 'I have no objection.'

Mitch was happy when his father spoke warmly like that.

Time seemed to pass more and more quickly. Mitch was endlessly busy doing his schoolwork, tending the garden, tidying his room, cleaning out the shed where Bugle slept and the pelicans' home in the old chook-house. His responsibilities weren't just three birds. All kinds of other duties kept increasing day by day.

There was no further news of Hardy Blight. 'Perhaps his buggy has broken down,' Fos said wryly. 'Or maybe he's fixed his engine so that he doesn't have to use so much oil any more.' Talk like that made Mitch uneasy. The problem of Hardy Blight never seemed to go away.

From time to time Mitch was still able to go out in his boat. Bugle and the pelicans knew the routine so well that they were waiting for him down at the landing as soon as he walked out of the house.

When he was out on the Coorong they sat in their special places in the boat although some-times all three of them took off and cruised about overhead for a while. Mitch liked to look up at them, marvelling at the differences in their flight — the pelicans flapping and gliding, flapping and gliding, like heavy cargo carriers, the swan like a feathered arrow. 'Swans are fast,' his father often said. 'They can reach speeds of 80 kilometres an hour.'

But whether the time they spent in the air was long or short they had an uncanny way of knowing when Mitch was about to pack up. He had barely started to pull up the pick when they came gliding down to join him on the trip home. It was a sight that fascinated the locals so much that Mitch was afraid the tourist invasion would start again.

Winter passed and the warm days of spring followed quickly. They didn't bring many tourists, but they brought back something much worse — Hardy Blight and Jimmy Small. Whiskers Burns told Mitch's father that he had seen them in the sandhills one day, and Wheelie Eels said they had roared past the roadhouse and given him a raspberry salute. Mitch was terrified that he would meet Hardy again, or that he might have to be a witness in a case against him. Somehow their lives always seemed to be colliding.

In September worries of that kind were joined by new fears — the first hints of huge changes that were waiting to carry Mitch away from his home and his happy life on the Coorong, perhaps for ever. One day he overheard his mother talking to Mrs Penn, who had come down to see Mitch at the beginning of the final term.

'We have to make a decision soon,' his mother said. 'Foster and I have been talking about it for weeks.'

'About high school?' Mrs Penn asked.

'Yes. Which one to choose, and how to arrange it.'

Mitch crept closer to the door, straining to hear every word.

'Mitchell is a good student. He simply must go to high school.'

Mitch's face flushed when he heard Mrs Penn's praise, but he was worried sick by what they were saying. After all, it was his life they were talking about.

'Foster has a brother in the city,' his mother went on. 'He and his wife were down here for a holiday last Christmas. They say Mitch could stay with them. Their own children have grown up.'

'That would be ideal.'

'They live in Marryatville.'

'Splendid. I'll gather the details of two or three schools that are within easy reach and send them to you. Then you and Foster can sit down with Mitch and talk it over with him before you decide. It would be a good idea to enrol him as soon as you can.'

There was silence for a while and then Mitch heard his mother sigh. 'He's going to miss all this — the Coorong, the birds, the lifestyle. And we're going to miss him more than I can say.'

'Of course.'

'He's going to be terribly homesick in the city. He'll hate it.'

'Most kids are homesick at first, but he'll get over it.'

'I doubt if Mitch ever will. He'll have to come back here permanently to be really happy.'

'Perhaps he will some day. Perhaps he'll be a ranger like his father.'

'That would be his dream.'

There was another pause. 'Who will look after the birds?' Mrs Penn asked.

'I will. They're going to miss him as much as he'll miss them. Especially Bugle.'

'Yes.'

'Mitch will be devastated. It will break his heart.'

Mitch couldn't bear to hear any more. He crept away from the door and sat down on the verandah, with the Coorong stretching away before him. His eyes misted with tears and a great sob welled up in his throat.

A few days later his father came home with surprising news. Thieves had raided the boats again, stealing petrol and all kinds of things from the cabins, but this time a trap was laid for them and they'd been caught red-handed.

Mitch was excited. 'Hardy Blight and Jimmy Small?'

His father shook his head. 'No.'

Mitch couldn't believe it. 'Who then?'

'Two break-and-enter criminals from the city. They've been raiding country towns for almost a year. They've confessed to twenty-five robberies.'

'But everyone was sure it was Hardy Blight.'

'They thought so. But there was no evidence.

It shows how dangerous it is to jump to conclusions, Mitch.'

His father paused for a moment. It was clear that he was choosing his words carefully. 'It will bring up questions about Wheelie's oil again — whether it really was Hardy Blight who took it.'

'But it was, Dad. I'm certain.'

'Did you actually see him?'

'Yes.'

'Take the oil and walk away with it?'

'Well, no. Not walk away with it. But I saw his hands as plain as anything.'

'They could have been anyone's hands. You'd need fingerprints to prove that they belonged to Hardy.'

'But there wasn't anyone else who could have done it.'

'You think so because you didn't see anyone. But a different person altogether could have parked out the back and walked round the corner of the roadhouse.'

Mitch was hurt. Nobody wanted to believe him, not even his own father. 'Well, I know what I saw,' he said stubbornly. 'It was Hardy Blight stealing two cans of oil for his buggy. I'll swear to it.'

His father answered gravely. 'If Hardy Blight is innocent, and if he gets wind of what you've just said, you may really have to swear to it — in court.'

'But, Dad …'

'I'm not denying what you saw, Mitch, but I want you to be very careful about what you make of it.'

By now Mitch was so confused that he hardly knew what to make of it himself. He wished he had never visited Whiskers Burns, never had a puncture, never gone to the roadhouse for help, never seen Hardy Blight or anyone else.

Sixteen

In October there was a public holiday and a long weekend. Mitch had been working so hard, finishing his assignments and preparing for his final assessments, that he was glad to have a break. Even his mother agreed that he deserved a few days off.

On Saturday morning he decided that the first thing he should do was to collect enough cockles from the ocean beach to last for the rest of the weekend. Because of the holiday his father was home for a change. He called out as Mitch jumped off the verandah on his way to the boat. 'Be careful. Remember the rules.'

'Yes, Dad.'

'And watch out for snakes,' his mother added. 'The warm weather is bringing them out.'

'Yes, Mum.'

'Have you packed your water bottle and lunch box?'

'Yes.'

'Enough petrol in the outboard?'

'I filled the tank last night.'

'OK. have a good day.'

When Mitch reached the landing, Plenty Full, Plenty Empty and Bugle were already waiting by the boat as usual. They had read his mind again and knew what he was about to do.

The pelicans snickered and snackered happily with their beaks. It sounded like dry sticks rattling in the wind. Bugle was already standing in the bow, and as the boat got under way he spread his wings for a moment and leaned forward with his neck stretched out in his favourite figurehead pose. As they sailed across the Coorong Mitch wondered whether he looked like a Chinese fisherman setting out with three birds trained to catch fish for him.

When they reached the far shore Mitch jumped out and carried the pick forward until the mooring rope was taut, and then pressed the tines deep into the sand with his foot, even though there was no likelihood that the boat would drag the anchor because the water was as still as glass. He picked up the hessian bag he always used for the cockles, dropped in his water bottle, and slung the bag over his shoulder. 'Come on, you lazy lot,' he said to the birds. 'Are you coming with me or are you going to sit here all day?'

Plenty Full and Plenty Empty eyed him as though they had been insulted and then took off and flew away deliberately towards the ocean beach. Bugle also rose but instead of following them he circled above Mitch, flying fast and low overhead for three or four minutes until he decided that Mitch was plodding along more slowly than a snail. Quite suddenly he straightened up and flew across the peninsula like a dart. By the time Mitch reached the beach all three birds were waiting for him. Bugle came forward, crooning happily. He seemed to be saying, 'I'm glad you've made it but you took forever. In future why don't you fly?'

Mitch sat down and took a long swig from his water bottle before starting to collect cockles. He had timed the trip well. The tide was out and he was able to walk about ankle deep in water, probing the sand with his bare hands. The cockles lay in patches. They were so big and smooth that he liked the feel of their shells as his hand closed over them. Within fifteen minutes he decided that he had gathered enough of them. There was no point in going on until his bag was so heavy that he would have to dump some of them on the way back. That would be the sort of criminal waste that would send his father into a fury.

Mitch lumped his load up the beach and sat down beyond the highwater mark to have another drink. Poking about in salt water always made him thirsty. At that point the two pelicans decided that they had put up with enough of Mitch's pointless time-wasting. Although they had waited for him politely he hadn't caught a single fish. They turned to face the breeze, spread their wings, and rose up so effortlessly that Mitch was rapt. As soon as they were airborne they turned and headed across the sandhills back to the Coorong. He gazed after them until their shapes dwindled away. 'See you later,' he called jokingly. 'Don't hurry.'

He stood up, seized his bag, and set off after them. He expected Bugle to fly off too, perhaps to have lunch on a patch of widgeon grass, but instead he circled overhead again, as he had earlier in the day, before heading back to the boat. Mitch felt strangely happy at the thought of the swan flying above him like an aerial patrol guarding him against danger.

And there was danger. By the time he had almost crossed the peninsula he was tired out. He was dragging his feet and the cockles seemed to be getting heavier by the minute. Once he stumbled and fell forward with his chin in the sand. As he staggered to his feet he didn't notice the snake ahead of him until he almost trod on it. He reeled back in sudden fear.

It was a red-bellied black, common enough around the Coorong. Although he had often seen them, he had never come so close to being bitten.

The snake had been sunning itself in a warm dip in the sand, enjoying the burst of spring weather after its long winter sleep. Mitch moved back cautiously, concentrating hard. After its first sudden reaction — its raised head and threatening attitude — it calmed down and started to glide away. Mitch watched warily. He still felt cold from shock but he was fascinated by the way it moved, curving and weaving like a stream of black molten glass flowing over a bed of glowing coals. It was one of the most beautiful creatures he had ever seen. Beautiful but dangerous. He eased back further and watched the snake disappear into a patch of bushy growth thirty metres away. Then he took a deep breath and walked on watchfully. His father was right. Sometimes among the sandhills danger leapt out at you so suddenly that it took you unawares.

Seventeen

When he reached the boat Bugle was waiting for him, but instead of standing in the bow as usual he was moving about on the shore. He seemed to be agitated. Mitch was concentrating on him so much that for a moment he didn't notice anything else. But when he turned to toss the bag of cockles into the boat he stopped short. He was stunned. The boat had sunk. The stern with the outboard on it was completely under water and the centre of the boat was partly covered. Only the bow was clear because the boat was sloping upwards on the sandy part of the shore.

Mitch blinked and looked again. What on earth had happened? How could the boat possibly sink in a place like this? The water was as calm as a baby's bath and the shore was soft sand. If it had happened on the other side of the Coorong he would have understood because there the shore was a jumble of jagged limestone as sharp as teeth. But not here.

He walked forward to the boat and leaned far over, bracing his hands on the rowlock while he tried to peer through the murk at the floor of the boat. There appeared to be a blemish there but it was hard to be certain. He stood back and eyed the boat again. Bugle came up beside him and gazed too, his long neck curving and his head on one side. 'What do you reckon, Bugle?' Mitch said. 'What's happened to our boat?'

At first he wondered whether he could bail the boat dry but realised that it was impossible. He didn't have a bailing bucket — nothing but a bait tin so small that he would have to bail constantly for a week to make any impression. In any case the water would probably leak in faster than he could bail it out. And the outboard motor was under the water and would be quite useless until it had been cleaned and dried out thoroughly.

What to do?

Slowly he began to see that his predicament was much worse than he had thought. He was alone on the far side of the Coorong. How was he going to get back home without a boat? He would be mad to try to swim across it. He was not a strong swimmer and the distance was too great. He would probably drown from exhaustion or cramp before he was halfway across.

To try to walk home was just as impossible. He would have to trudge all the way down to the far end of the south lagoon, plough his way through the stinking ooze there, and walk back up the landward side. How far would that be? Sixty, seventy, eighty kilometres? It would take him a whole day. Maybe two days. There were no walking tracks so he would have to blunder along over sandhills and soaks, through scrubs and bushes. Ridiculous. Impossible.

It might be possible to cross the Coorong further down at a spot called The Narrows or Hell's Gate where the two shores came close together, but it would still mean such a long walk that he would be exhausted by the time he reached it, and the water was deeper there. And even if he managed to get across he would still have a long walk up the landward side again.

He had to admit that he was marooned. It frightened him. What would his father and mother be thinking as each hour passed without any sign of him? He sat down by the boat, trying to think. Bugle came over to him and started probing about in his pockets for radishes or tidbits. Mitch smiled sadly and rubbed his neck. 'Sorry Bugle,' he said. 'There's nothing. Nothing at all.'

Mitch tried to remember the things that his father kept saying about care and safety. If something goes wrong stay where you are unless it's very dangerous there. Keep to the place you said you were going to. Don't start wandering off into the mulga where nobody will even think of looking for you. Always carry something to help searchers find you — matches to light a fire and send up a smoke signal, a small mirror to flash a beam of bright light, a white cloth or handkerchief to wave or stand on a stick. But above all, stay where you are. Send a message if you can.'

'OK,' Mitch decided. 'I'll send a message.'

He didn't have any matches or a mirror but he had a white shirt. He took it off and examined it. It was rather grubby but he thought it would do to attract attention if he fixed it to a stick and waved it about above his head. He went over to the boat and groped about under the water in the stern until he found his fishing box. He carried it up onto the bank, took out his filleting knife, and cut a metre of nylon line from one of his reels. After that he seized one of the oars, tied his shirt to one end, and held it up as high as he could. Presto! He had made himself an emergency signal to wave above his head.

Unfortunately there was no-one to see it except Bugle who twisted his neck and gazed up at it, completely puzzled. His gaze suggested that Mitch had gone crazy because oars were meant to dip and splash in the water, not stand up in the air with shirts on the end of them.

It wasn't long before Mitch realised that the idea was hopeless. He wasn't strong enough to keep waving the signal for more than a minute or two, and the odds of anyone seeing it in that time were like a lottery. Even his father and mother would have trouble pin-pointing it from the verandah of the house unless they were scouring the peninsula with big binoculars.

A fisherman or a group of tourists sailing on the Coorong would be more likely to see him, especially if he danced about, shouting and waving, but there was no boat in sight. Several of them had been out earlier in the day but they had headed for home. Mitch looked around and guessed why. A bank of clouds had appeared low on the horizon and was gradually moving up the western sky. He had learned enough about clouds to know that a weather front was on its way. No doubt the skippers of the boats had been listening to the forecasts on the radio and had run for shelter. The Coorong could be a nasty place in a big blow.

He took the oar and stood it upright in the sand, then stepped back and looked at it critically. It was pathetic. He was sure nobody would ever see it. For a while he sat with his elbows on his knees and gazed across at his house. It seemed near enough, yet for all the hope he had of reaching it he might as well have been sitting in the middle of the Sahara Desert. Bugle seemed depressed too. After plodding about for a few minutes he sat down and waited for things to return to normal.

Mitch turned to him sadly and rubbed his neck. 'I'm sorry, Bugle,' he said. 'I'm stuck here. You'd better leave me. You can be home in a couple of minutes. You can fly.'

He sat up sharply almost before he had finished the last word. 'Yes, you can fly. You can take a message.' But his excitement died down as quickly as it had started. He had nothing he could use for a message even if he could persuade Bugle to carry it. There was no paper in his fishing box, and if there had been it would have turned into pulp by now. He didn't have a pen or pencil either.

He stood up and Bugle stood up beside him. He seemed to be getting restless, fed up with Mitch's antics. But Mitch was thinking hard. An idea was forming in his mind that was not so hopeless after all, but it would depend on Bugle to succeed. Absolutely on Bugle.

He pulled the oar out of the sand, untied his shirt, and cut off a small part of the sleeve with the knife — a tiny piece no more than ten or twelve centimetres square. Then he turned and ran back into the sandhills as fast as he could. His sudden movements alarmed Bugle so much that he took off and flew about uncertainly overhead. Mitch looked up at him, desperately afraid that he had finally given up and decided to go home.

'Stay, Bugle,' Mitch called. 'Stay. Stay with me.'

Mitch ran until he came to the place where Hardy Blight and his offsiders had spent the night around their campfire. He scratched about urgently, looking for charcoal and the blackened ends of small sticks. It wasn't hard to find them. Within a minute or two he had collected half a dozen and was on his way back to the boat, panting so hard that he had to stop to regain his breath. Bugle was still confused by Mitch's antics and flew about uncertainly before landing again. Mitch was greatly relieved and rubbed his neck gratefully. 'Good boy,' he said. 'Good boy, Bugle. You stay.'

Mitch spread the piece of cloth on the lid of his fishing box and stretched it as tightly as he could while he wrote on it with his charcoal sticks. S O S he scrawled painstakingly in sooty black, followed by M I T C H. There was no need for anything else. There wasn't space for a longer message anyway. His mother and father knew where he had gone. If they received the message — and that was the vital question — they would automatically come looking for him in the right place.

He took the cloth and a bit of fishing line and went over to Bugle. For a minute he patted him and talked to him gently while he tied the cloth around his neck. He had to be careful. If it was too loose it would slip off, but if it was too tight it would be in danger of choking the messenger.

He tugged on the corner of the cloth several times to make sure that it was firm, then lifted Bugle and stood him in his favourite spot on the bow of the boat so that he could use it as a launching platform. 'Go, Bugle', he called. 'Go home now. Go, go, go.'

Bugle hesitated. Mitch couldn't blame him for thinking that the world had gone mad, but he kept on urging him to take off. 'Home now, Bugle. Go home now. Time for radishes.' Bugle didn't really know what he was supposed to do but in the end he was probably fed up with all the nonsense and simply flew off.

Mitch watched eagerly at the shape with the strong wings and out-thrust neck flying across the water. He could only hope that Bugle would land near the house somewhere and that someone would see him and wonder what was tied around his neck.

Eighteen

It was the oncoming storm as much as Bugle's message that helped to rescue Mitch. His father was always aware of the weather. He knew all its moods and he knew how suddenly and fiercely they could change.

'Mitch should be home by now,' he said uneasily. 'There's a big blow coming. The barometer has gone into free-fall.'

Mitch's mother was even more worried. 'I hope nothing has gone wrong.'

Mr Bird took his binoculars out to the verandah and scanned the Coorong. He adjusted the focus and moved his gaze slowly back and forth over the far shore and the sandhills. Now and then he glanced anxiously at the sky. The clouds were blue-black.

Just then Plenty Full and Plenty Empty came gliding down towards the house. They landed gracefully near the boat jetty and waddled up towards their roosting corner in the old chook-shed. Mr Bird grunted. 'They know what's coming all right. All the birds do. So why doesn't Mitch?' He knew the danger. If Mitch was caught in the middle of the Coorong when the storm struck his little dinghy would never survive. It would be swamped instantly.

He raised the binoculars again and concentrated on part of the shore where Mitch usually moored his boat. As he did so he checked himself and looked again. A bird was flying over the water towards him — a black swan travelling very fast and growing clearer by the second. A hundred metres away it banked with a flash of its white flight feathers and came in to land near the verandah.

It was Bugle. Bugle with a piece of white cloth tied around his black neck.

For a moment Mitch's father wondered whether the swan had been hurt and whether someone had tied a bandage around the wound, but then he realised what it was. Although he had never been fond of Mitch's birds and had none of the warm friendship with them that Mitch had, he was not a stranger either. He moved forward cautiously and held out his hand. He was tense and anxious, afraid that Bugle would back away or, worse still, fly off in fright.

'Here Bugle,' he said. 'Good boy, Bugle.'

The swan retreated uncertainly. Mitch's father took a step forward, coaxing and urging. Bugle sensed his impatience and retreated again. It was maddening. If the cloth around his neck really was a message then every second was important. 'Come here, Bugle,' he called. 'Come, come, come,' but his tone was so urgent that it unsettled Bugle more than ever.

Luckily Mitch's mother came out just then. 'What's going on?' she asked.

'It's Bugle. Something is tied around his neck but he won't let me touch it.'

'Stand back a bit,' she said. 'Let me try.'

She moved forward slowly, making soft crooning noises and holding out her hand. Bugle took a step forward and eyed her trustingly. She was a friend who often fed him if Mitch was busy. Within a second or two she was at his side rubbing his neck and untying the message. She glanced at it and looked up urgently. 'It's from Mitch. An SOS. Hurry. He needs help.'

Mr Bird leaped from the verandah, ran down to the landing, and sprang into the patrol boat that was always moored there. A moment later it was surging across the Coorong with the engine at full throttle and the bow cutting the water like a destroyer.

As soon as Mitch caught sight of it he grabbed his shirt and waved it furiously. He was relieved to see his father change course slightly and head straight for him. Fifty metres out he throttled back and came in carefully near the sunken dinghy. 'Are you OK,' he yelled.

'Yes, Dad.'

'What happened?'

'The dinghy sank.'

'Why?'

'Sprang a leak.'

'How?'

'Don't know. It was lying here like this when I came back from the beach.'

His father had one eye on Mitch and one on the sky. 'There's no time to fix it now. The storm's almost here. Wade out, holding on to the dinghy. I'll come inshore as far as I can. See if you can haul yourself aboard.'

Mitch managed it, but not before slipping into deep water and giving himself a dunking. He crawled over to the wheelhouse and stood up, streaming with water. His father glanced at him briefly to see that he was OK, then swung the boat round, pushed the throttle hard, and raced back the way he had come. He kept glancing over his shoulder at the western sky, leaning forward over the wheel as if urging the boat to go faster.

They barely made it. The first blast of the storm struck them just as they were coming in to the landing in front of the house. Mitch's mother who had been watching anxiously raced down to grab the mooring rope. As Mitch threw it to her he was almost blown overboard by a second blast. 'Quick, quick,' she cried, but her voice was lost in the fury of the wind and the first fierce onrush of rain.

Mitch's father hastily battened down the boat and leaped onto the jetty. 'Run!' he yelled. 'Up to the house. Go for your life!'

They dashed forward, the rain stinging their faces and their bodies bent forward against the force of the gale. When they reached the shelter of the verandah Meg put her arms around Mitch and hugged him. 'You're safe,' she said fervently. 'Thank God you're safe.'

Mitch had a special question to ask.

'Was it Bugle? Was it Bugle who warned you with his message?'

She smiled happily. 'Yes, yes. He came right up to us on the verandah.'

'Did you pat him and thank him?'

'Of course. And I gave him a special treat as a reward.'

Mitch looked around. 'Where is he now?'

'In his favourite place in the workshop, as snug as a gosling.'

'And Plenty Full and Plenty Empty?'

'Both in the chook-shed.'

Mitch was happy. 'Good. Then everything's OK.'

His father looked out at the Coorong where streaming whitecaps were being lashed by the gale. 'Not quite,' he said. 'There's still a dinghy and an expensive outboard lying over there under the water.'

Nineteen

The storm raged all through Saturday night and most of Sunday. 'What a waste of a long weekend,' Mitch grumbled. 'If I can't go fishing tomorrow the pelicans are going to starve.'

'There won't be any fishing tomorrow,' his father answered bluntly. 'We have to salvage the dinghy, remember. If we don't fix it tomorrow we'll never be able to do it. I go back to work on Tuesday.'

'And so do you my boy,' Mitch's mother said sternly. 'Nose to the grindstone every minute of the day. Your final assessments are due next month.'

Mitch looked in the kitchen mirror and grimaced at himself. 'That's just great,' he said.

Luckily the storm blew itself out on Sunday night. Monday morning dawned so fine and clear that Mr Bird was up early, urging Mitch to hurry. By seven o'clock they were on their way across the Coorong. Bugle travelled with them but Plenty Full and Plenty Empty trailed above them like a pair of living kites.

As soon as they reached the peninsula Mr Bird waded ashore and examined the dinghy. It was more waterlogged then ever because it had been hammered by strong waves during the storm. He disconnected the outboard and floundered over to the patrol boat with it. 'That's going to be a nice little job for you,' he said, 'to dry this thing and get it going again.'

He waded back and stood near the stern of the dinghy. 'Take a good grip on the bow,' he called, 'and push as hard as you can. Between us we have to try to roll it over.'

It was not as hard as Mitch thought. He realised how strong his father really was because he heaved the dinghy on its side with a hefty lift and they both slid it up onto the sand clear of the water. There they tipped it upside down and bent over the keel, looking for the leak that had caused all the trouble. The hole was actually quite small, but certainly big enough to send the water spurting up into the boat and sinking it.

After a while Mitch's father straightened up, still eyeing the hole. 'It would need a very sharp rock to do a thing like that. A jagged piece of limestone maybe. Or a lump of metal. And you'd have to hit it pretty hard.' He looked at Mitch questioningly. 'Are you sure you didn't run into something?'

Mitch was hurt because it sounded like an accusation. 'No I didn't,' he answered firmly. 'The boat was quite OK on the trip over. There wasn't a drop of water in it. It must have happened here.' He waved his hand all about. 'But this shore is soft sand. There's not a stone anywhere, not even a pebble. So how did it happen?'

His father stepped back with a grim expression. 'In that case there's only one answer. It must have been done purposely by someone while you were over at the beach.'

Mitch was shocked. 'Done purposely?'

'Yes.'

'But who?'

His father shrugged but didn't answer.

'And why? Why would anyone want to do a thing like that?'

'Because of a grudge, maybe. Someone who thinks you are to blame for something.'

Mitch couldn't believe it. 'You mean revenge?'

'Something like that.'

'But that's …' Mitch stopped suddenly and stared. 'D'you reckon it was Hardy Blight?'

'You mustn't say that,' his father answered sternly. 'You can think what you like but you can't say it. There's absolutely no evidence. The boat may not have been damaged by human beings at all.'

Mitch was sure that someone had done it but as usual there was no evidence. Without proof it was all dangerous guesswork or silent suspicion.

'Come on,' his father called brusquely. 'We have to mend this tub and get it back home.'

He waded out to the patrol boat and returned

with the tool kit. After a couple of attempts he managed to shape a plug that fitted the hole and then set it with sealer to bond it firmly and make it waterproof, at least for the time being. Bugle stood nearby all the time, taking a keen interest in everything that was going on, but Plenty Full and Plenty Empty flew over to the patrol boat and stood supervising from the top of the wheelhouse.

Mr Bird saw them and turned to Mitch sharply. 'Get them away from there. That's a Government boat. I don't want birds messing all over it.'

Mitch pretended to be hurt. 'They don't mess.'

His father scoffed. 'No? Just take a look at the place where they roost. You should know. You have to clean it up every other day.'

'I'll shift them as soon as we get going.'

'Well that's right now. We'll tow the dinghy as carefully as we can. And let's hope it doesn't sink when we're halfway across.'

They righted the dinghy and hitched it onto the stern of the big boat, at the same time telling the pelicans that it was time for them to go.

'Keep an eye on it,' Mitch's father called. 'Yell if it starts to take water.'

All went well. Within half an hour they were back at their own landing. Fos carried the outboard ashore and laid it on a clean sheet of plastic. 'Your job,' he said to Mitch. 'Clean and dry it thoroughly, then oil and grease it and we'll see if it still works.'

He went back to the dinghy and reinforced the mend so that it would never leak again. Mitch was happy. It wasn't often that they could do things together like a couple of mates. Better still, they were successful. When they put the outboard back on the dinghy it started at once and ran smoothly. They smiled at each other. 'Time for a bite,' his father said, and they walked up to the house side by side.

Twenty

If Mitch thought he could relax for the rest of the day he was wrong. They had just finished lunch. His mother was looking for something on the Internet and his father had gone into his study to finish some paperwork, when Mitch suddenly remembered something. 'Oh blast!' he cried.

His mother looked up with a frown. 'What now?'

'I've left my fishing box over there.'

'How on earth did you come to do that?'

'I took it from the boat to get my knife and nylon line for Bugle's message. I didn't even think of it when we were over there this morning. It's been lying in the sand all the weekend, unless someone's nicked it.'

'You should be more careful with your things.'

'I'll have to go back and get it. My two good reels are in it, and all my hooks and lines and stuff.'

His mother was having trouble finding what she wanted. She looked up impatiently from the keyboard. 'Oh all right then. Go over and get it.' She called after him as he disappeared through the doorway. 'But come straight back. We don't want any more SOS messages from you.' Mitch was outside by now and didn't catch her comment. Bugle was already waiting for him down at the boat. As usual, he knew what Mitch was about to do.

It was an anxious crossing. Although the outboard had run well enough when they had tested it at the landing it started to splutter and cough so badly out on the water that Mitch was terrified it was going to cut out altogether. 'Come on,' he urged. 'Don't you dare pack up out here.' He could imagine the agony if he had to row back all the way home against the breeze with heavy oars and blistered hands.

The motor seemed to hear him. After hiccoughing for a minute or two it settled down and ran smoothly for the rest of the way. 'Just a sore throat after two days in the water,' Mitch told himself. He anchored the boat temporarily while he went ashore to look for his fishing box. Bugle jumped ashore too and stood watching as if wondering why Mitch kept coming back to this particular spot. What was so special about it?

At first Mitch couldn't find the fishing box. He prospected back and forth, unable to remember exactly where he had put it. 'Don't tell me someone's nicked it already,' he muttered to himself. 'Those reels cost a fortune.'

In the end he stumbled on it by good luck

rather than good sense. The handle and part of the lid were just visible above the sand. The storm had almost buried it. He knelt down and started to dig it out with his bare hands when Bugle suddenly honked in alarm and moved away restlessly, gazing up at the sandhills behind them. Mitch sat back on his heels and looked at him. 'What's up, Bugle?' he called. Bugle honked again, more alarmed than ever. Mitch was uneasy. 'What is it, Bugle? What's wrong?'

Then he heard it — an engine in the distance, revving hard and coming through the sandhills. A dune buggy! The tone of the engine told Mitch what it was doing — easing off when the buggy plunged down into a hollow at one minute and rising to a howl as it crawled up a steep slope at the next. It seemed to be coming straight towards them. Before long it was no more than a hundred metres away. Mitch stood up hastily and turned to face it. Bugle gave a final honk of alarm and took off, flying in a wide arc over the water.

The dune buggy suddenly rose up against the skyline on the crest of the high dune above Mitch. For an instant he glimpsed the driver, a big man with a black beard — Hardy Blight without a doubt. All kinds of fears surged about in his mind. Was Hardy coming back to see if someone had mended the dinghy? Had he seen Mitch crossing the Coorong a few minutes earlier and come to take revenge for the rumours about Wheelie's oil? Did he plan to vent his anger on Mitch simply because he was the ranger's kid?

For a second or two the buggy ploughed along the top of the sandhill with its engine roaring. No-one ever knew what caused the terrible catastrophe in the next few seconds. Perhaps Hardy Blight caught sight of Mitch with a shock and lost control, for the buggy veered without warning. As it did so the downward side of the crest gave way in a sandy avalanche, the offside wheels dropped sharply and the buggy tilted. Mitch had a split-second picture of the driver wrenching the steering wheel, trying to slew his way back onto level sand again. It simply made things worse. The buggy was already teetering at an angle and the sudden wrench did the rest. In an instant it rolled over, somersaulting faster and faster down the face of the sandhill towards the Coorong below.

Mitch had no time to think as the hurtling buggy came cartwheeling down towards him. His legs were as rigid as sticks, as they were in nightmares when he desperately wanted to run away but found that he couldn't move.

Near the bottom of the sandhill the catapulting buggy leaped once more in a wild somersault, swung slightly to the left, and skidded towards the water. At the last second Mitch tried to leap away, but he was too late. The frame of the buggy struck him a sidelong blow as it passed, hurling him aside like a limp doll. He lay where he fell, silent and unconscious. The buggy skidded on for a few more metres and stopped at the edge of the Coorong, half in and half out of the water. The engine cut out, doused in a cloud of steam. The frame, with Hardy Blight's unconscious body still held by his seat belt, lay unsteadily at an angle, in danger of slipping under and drowning him if he was not dead already.

A great silence hung over the place. There was no sound, no movement — nothing to alert anyone that a terrible tragedy had just happened. Mitch Bird and Hardy Blight were lying on the far shore of the Coorong. Nobody near at hand knew they were there. Nobody knew whether they were alive or dead.

Twenty-one

It was Bugle who broke the silence. After his first terrified escape from the sound of the dune buggy he had flown far out and landed on the water. He was restless and distressed, unable to understand what was going on. He missed Mitch and he didn't like swimming about on his own. Finally he took off and flew back to the scene of the accident but he didn't land. The buggy was too close to the dinghy.

He could see Mitch lying motionless on the sand. It was all strange and frightening. A deep instinct told him that something was very wrong. He rose higher and began flying in circles, honking loudly and once or twice bugling in a long note that carried far out over the water.

There was a boat at anchor further up the Coorong. Presently a head popped up from the cabin and swivelled about in the open air — a head with a beanie pulled down to its ears and an enormous beard on the face below it. Whiskers Burns.

Whiskers climbed out and made his way to the bow to pull up his anchor. Half way there he paused and listened. A sound was coming to him faintly on the breeze. A bird sound. A swan honking and bugling. He looked about, squinting against the light, trying to find the place it was coming from. For a while he couldn't pinpoint it but then the bird banked and he caught the shape of its big wings and the sudden flash of its flight feathers. A black swan, flying in circles and behaving strangely. He stood watching for a minute longer, then gave up and bent to haul in the anchor. Birds did unusual things. It was part of life in the wild.

When the anchor was up he wiped his wet hands on his shirt and looked about again. The swan was still flying round and round at the same spot, still calling. He was curious. Perhaps he should go and take a look. It would only take a few minutes. Perhaps one of its cygnets was in trouble. Although Whiskers disliked pelicans, he had a soft spot for swans.

He started the engine and headed down the Coorong towards the shore where the swan was circling. As he neared it he saw a dinghy moored near by and put two and two together. The dinghy belonged to the ranger's son and the bird was the tame swan that followed him everywhere. Something had happened to upset it. A moment later he caught sight of the dune buggy lying on its side partly under water and drew in his breath. 'Holy honkers,' he whispered. A man was lying in the buggy, still held by his seat belt. He knew who it was. Hardy Blight, unconscious or dead.

Whiskers cut his engine, ran the bow of his boat in to the sandy shore, and threw out the anchor. Although he was seventy years old he was still strong and agile, used to carrying heavy boxes of fish and handling the boat on his own.

He jumped from the bow and hurried towards Hardy Blight. It was only then that he saw Mitch and stopped short, his breath hissing. 'God, oh God,' he murmured. He ran over and knelt beside Mitch, feeling for his pulse. It was hard for his horny fingers to detect a heart-beat but after a moment he could see that Mitch was still breathing. There was a terrible bruise on the side of his head but no blood. He was still alive.

He left Mitch lying where he was and ran over to the dune buggy. After examining him for a minute he decided that Hardy was also alive but badly hurt. Blood was oozing from wounds in his head and arms, and his legs were twisted at an angle in the wreckage.

It was impossible to work out what had happened. Had the boy been riding in the buggy with Hardy Blight? That was impossible. Had Blight purposely tried to run him down? Surely he wouldn't do a thing like that. But there was no time to guess or ask questions. He clambered back onto his boat and hurried to his radio. Although it was a public holiday he managed to get through and stammered out his message urgently and breathlessly.

'There's been an accident. On the shore of the Coorong. The Bird boy and Hardy Blight. Both hurt bad. Unconscious.' He halted his rush of words for a second to answer puzzled questions. 'Who am I? Does it matter, for God's sake? Burns. Yes Burns. Where am I? On the bloody Coorong, don't you know. On the far side. The peninsula. Opposite the Bird house. Bird. Yes, Bird. No, not bird. Fos Bird. The ranger. Get onto him straight away. Tell him to come across as fast as he can.' Whiskers stopped to catch his breath, frustrated that it was so hard to send a simple message. 'Oh, and call an ambulance,' he added. Tell 'em to drive to the ranger's house. What? Of course it's urgent. You got all that?' He paused again and repeated the essence of the message, suspicious that everything was going to be garbled and misunderstood.

He put back the microphone and stroked his beard. Lifting heavy weights every day was no problem but trying to send a few simple instructions left him exhausted.

There were still other things to do. He grabbed his First Aid kit from the locker on his boat and went ashore again. There didn't seem to be anything he could do for Mitch but he needed to stop the flow of blood from Hardy's wounds. He took two or three antiseptic patches from the kit, placed them carefully over the wounds and wrapped them in thick bandages. There wasn't much more that he could do. He wanted to pull Hardy out of the buggy in case it slid further into the water but he hesitated for fear of doing even more damage to his wounds or broken bones.

He went back to Mitch again. Apart from the blue bruise on his head there were no wounds that he could see, although that didn't mean much if Mitch had concussion or brain damage. He took a small folded towel from the kit, lifted Mitch's head clear of the sand, and gently pushed the towel under it. After that he could only wait.

It was while he was sitting there quietly that he heard soft sounds behind him. He turned quickly. Bugle was standing a few metres away, gazing at Mitch. Every now and then he crooned sadly. Whiskers wondered whether it was his way of crying. 'What's the matter?' Whiskers asked. 'Are you worried about your mate? He'll be OK. We'll get him to hospital as soon as we can.'

Bugle settled down and honked softly. And so they sat there together, the old man and the black swan, waiting for the rescue that was a long time coming.

Twenty-Two

When the message reached them Mitch's father and mother ran headlong down to the landing and leapt onto the patrol boat. In a few seconds it was racing across the Coorong even faster than it had two days earlier when it was escaping from the storm. Whiskers saw them coming and waved frantically.

As soon as they landed they rushed forward,

distraught at the sight of Mitch's limp body. There was confusion for a while, with many questions and no answers, but the urgent task was to get Mitch and Hardy onto the boat and to ferry them over to the house as quickly as they could.

It was a difficult and dangerous job. Without Whiskers it would have been impossible. He and Fos lifted Mitch tenderly and carried him between them, first wading through the water and finally hoisting him onto the boat where his mother settled him down under a warm blanket. 'Hurry,' she whispered as the men went back to get Hardy. 'Hurry, hurry.'

This time things were much more difficult. Hardy was a heavy man and he had to be extricated from the wreck of the buggy without further harm. In the end Meg joined the men and between the three of them they were able to lift him out cautiously and lie him down at the waterline. They rested there for a minute, afraid of the task that faced them next.

'We'll never be able to lift him up on to the patrol boat,' Fos said. 'Not standing up to our arm-pits in water with the deck higher than our heads.'

'What then?' Mrs Bird asked. 'We can't leave him here.'

'Only one way,' Whiskers answered. 'Put him in the boy's dinghy. Tow him behind the cutter.'

Mr Bird glanced at him admiringly. 'That's a shrewd idea.'

It didn't take long to carry Hardy into the dinghy and bed him down in it. Whiskers left his own boat where it was moored and travelled back with them. Meg was deeply grateful to the old man. 'Thank you,' she said fervently. 'Thank you for everything, especially for finding Mitch in the first place.'

Whiskers looked up and pointed. 'Look,' he said. 'Don't thank me. Thank that bird up there.' Bugle was flying above them, following the boat all the way back to the house. 'Without the swan I would never have found the boy and the man. They could have been lying there all day.'

Meg gazed up gratefully. 'Thank you, Bugle,' she said softly. 'Thank you, you wonderful bird.'

As they neared the shore they were thankful to see that two ambulance officers with stretchers were waiting on the landing. With four men to do the lifting it took only a few minutes to put Mitch and Hardy Blight into the ambulance. One officer drove while the other rode in the back with the two patients.

'We'll follow in the car,' Fos called. 'We want to be at the hospital when Mitch is admitted.'

'Of course.'

And so the little cavalcade raced off towards the city. Bugle followed. People who saw him pointed up in astonishment. 'Look, the swan is following the ambulance. Weird.'

Some knew about Mitch and his swan. 'Let's hope nothing has happened to the boy. If he's been hurt that bird will follow him.'

It wasn't until Bugle was far from the Coorong that he finally broke off his flight, banked sharply, and flew back home. But the house was empty and Mitch's dinghy was bobbing forlornly at the landing. Bugle couldn't understand why the world had been turned upside down so suddenly.

Meanwhile the ambulance sped on. Inside, Mitch and Hardy Blight lay side by side, unconscious and unknowing. In a strange way their feud had finally brought them together.

Twenty-three

*M*itch lay in a coma for three days, with his mother constantly at his bedside. When he opened his eyes at last he was bewildered, unable to understand where he was or what had happened to him. She rushed out to tell the doctors and nurses and then ran back to his bed and bent over him, 'Mitch,' she whispered. 'Mitch, it's me.'

Mitch looked up at her face for a long moment. 'Hi, Mum.'

A white-coated doctor came hurrying in and she turned to him joyfully. 'He's awake,' she said. 'And he's just recognised me.'

The doctor examined Mitch carefully, peering into his eyes and testing his reflexes. Finally he stood back and smiled. 'I think he's going to be OK. But it will take time.' Mitch gazed about at everything in the ward but when he tried to move he winced with pain. 'My leg hurts,' he said.

The doctor leaned forward again. 'It's in plaster, Mitch. It was broken in the accident.'

The word seemed to jolted Mitch's memory and he struggled to lift himself on his elbows. 'The dune buggy,' he cried. 'Hardy Blight.' His mother came forward quickly and pressed his hand. 'He's in another hospital — a hospital for grown-ups.'

'The dune buggy. What about the dune buggy?'

'It's still over there. Mr Small and his friends are going to try to save it.'

'Is Hardy Blight hurt?'

'Yes.'

'Bad?'

'We think so. We don't really know.'

She pressed his hand again and pushed back the hair from his forehead. 'You must rest now. Don't worry about all that.'

Mitch was given painkillers and it wasn't long before he drifted off to sleep.. His body seemed to be wrapped in cotton wool, as soft and warm as a cocoon.

As everyone was leaving, Mitch's father came running up the corridor. He had only just heard the news. Meg hugged him happily and the doctor stopped to reassure him. 'Yes, Mitchell has come out of it better than we could have expected. There's no permanent damage as far as we can see at this stage. We'll keep a close watch on him for a week or so. If everything is OK after that he can go home.'

Mitch's father was still anxious. 'What about his leg?'

'It's not a bad break. It should knit quite well.'

'How long will that take?'

'Eight or nine weeks. I'll arrange a pair of

crutches for him. He can practise using them here in hospital so that he can move about safely when he goes home. We'll keep in touch. When he's ready, the plaster can come off and hopefully he can get on with normal life again.'

Twenty-four

$\mathcal{M}$itch stayed in hospital for nine days. His mother and father visited him every afternoon, often with Uncle Harry and Aunt Nancy with whom they were staying while they were in the city. Mrs Penn also came, buoying him up with smiles, bringing books for him to read, and leaving gifts of chocolates on his bedside cabinet.

On the tenth morning his father arrived in

the Land Cruiser to take him home. A couple of orderlies from the hospital helped him aboard with his crutches, waved him goodbye and wished him luck.

As they drove off Mitch looked back. His mind was full of memories. 'I wonder how Hardy Blight is getting on,' he said. 'We haven't heard anything about him.'

His father looked at him earnestly. 'We've just had news. He died yesterday.'

Mitch was shocked. Although he had been frightened of Hardy Blight and had even had nightmares about him, the news left him numb, especially since he, Mitch, had been involved in the same accident and could have been killed too.

'It's sad,' his father said. 'What a waste of a life.'

Mitch sat thinking. 'If Hardy really did steal Wheelie's oil, and slash our tyres, and sink the dinghy, no-one will ever know, will they? Not now. It'll be a secret forever.'

His father waited for a long time before he answered. 'Yes,' he said at last. 'If he had any secrets he has carried them with him to the grave.'

He paused again. 'And that's where it's best for them to stay.'

For the rest of the long drive home Mitch sat staring silently through the windscreen, reliving the terrible events that had swept over him so swiftly. It wasn't until they were almost home that he roused himself.

'What about Bugle?' he asked anxiously. 'And Plenty Full and Plenty Empty?'

'The pelicans are still around. We're not likely to get rid of them.'

'And Bugle?'

'He hung about for a few days but then he disappeared.'

Mitch was indescribably sad. 'I'll bet Bugle was lonely. I'll bet he went off looking for me.'

'You're imagining things.'

'He was my best friend.'

'He'll be fending for himself, and that's a good thing. Wild creatures should live in the wild.'

'He wouldn't be alive at all if I hadn't saved him. He wouldn't even have hatched out of the egg.'

His father opened his mouth to answer but then decided against it. He was so grateful to be bringing Mitch back home that he didn't want to spoil it with an argument.

Mitch's mother was waiting outside for them when they arrived. She had put a big WELCOME HOME sign above the door and had prepared his favourite pie for lunch. As he eased himself out of the Land Cruiser on his crutches she ran forward and hugged him so hard that he almost toppled over. By the time they were inside together the place seemed ready for a party. He thought it really was worth a celebration just to be back home.

After a while he hopped out onto the verandah and leant back against the wall on his crutches. For a long time he stood looking out at the Coorong and the golden sandhills beyond it. He could pinpoint the place of the accident that had taken Hardy Blight's life and almost taken his own.

Twenty-five

Things seemed different now. The world was changing and would never be the same again — for him or anyone else. Although the doctor had said that his broken leg would be back to normal by Christmas, and although Mrs Penn was sure he would catch up the work he had missed and finish the year with a good report, he knew that a priceless part of his life was ending.

A new world was waiting for him in the new year and he was uneasy about it: high school with rules, timetables and new programs, classes of twenty or thirty kids instead of school days on his own, Uncle Harry and Aunt Nancy in place of his mother and father, the rush and noise of the city instead of the peace of the Coorong.

He was still thinking about it when he heard a sound that made him start forward and look up eagerly. It was a bugling call, once, twice, three times. An excited cry of joy. Then there was a rush of wide wings and a big black bird swept down and landed in front of him. Bugle was back home.

Mitch gave a great shout and hopped forward. His mother came hurrying out of the house, fearful that something had happened to him. He turned to her with shining eyes. 'Look, Mum,' he cried. 'It's Bugle. He's back.' But Bugle was not alone. Behind him, landing a little further back and then waiting shyly, was another swan. A companion. A female.

Mitch's mother smiled warmly. 'Look what he's brought back with him. While you were in hospital he found himself a mate. I'll go and get them both a treat.'

Bugle walked forward on the verandah. Mitch had tears in his eyes as he bent forward and stroked Bugle's neck in the old way. What secret instinct, he wondered, had told him that Mitch was back home.

He stroked Bugle's neck again. 'You're the best friend in the world,' he said softly. 'You're a magic bird.'

His mother returned with a handful of tidbits and offered some of them to Bugle. He crooned softly and snapped them up.

'What about your mate?' she said. 'Isn't she beautiful? A real princess.'

Mitch looked up quickly. 'That's a lovely name. Princess.'

'Yes it is.'

'Give me a few bits. I'll see if I can coax her.'

The new swan took a few steps forward but then stopped, afraid to come further. He threw a few bits over to her. She hesitated, then bent and ate them warily.

'She'll soon get to know us,' his mother said. 'Bugle will see to that.'

Mitch eyed her sadly. 'But I won't be here, not if I have to go to high school.'

'Then perhaps it's a good thing that Bugle has found a mate and discovered that you are not always here. He and the princess will be able to look after themselves.'

'But will they ever come back again?'

'Of course they will. Every time you're home on holidays they'll come to find you. They'll know.'

'Really?'

'Absolutely. And in time perhaps they will even bring a family of little cygnets with them.'

Mitch smiled. 'That would be fantastic.'

Bugle honked softly and waddled down to the landing, with Princess close behind. Mitch saw at once what Bugle had in mind. 'No,' he called. 'No rides in the boat today. Not until after Christmas. I've got a bung leg.'

Bugle stopped and looked back questioningly, but when he saw that Mitch was not following he accepted the fact that there would be no ride today. He stayed a little longer but finally took off, with the princess following close behind. Mitch saw the flash of their wings as they banked and flew away. He kept watching and watching until they dwindled into distant specks and faded from sight.

He sighed and moved off slowly on his crutches. 'I think I'll come inside and lie down for a while,' he said. 'The crutches hurt my armpits.'

'I'll go and get your bed ready,' his mother called back. 'The doctor said you should get plenty of rest.'

Mitch hopped along the verandah to the door, but before he opened it he turned and looked out once more at the long lagoon of the Coorong and the golden sandhills that would remain part of his life for ever. He was sad but resigned. Although his heart ached he was as ready to face the new world as he would ever be.